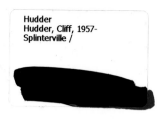

Splinterville

Splinterville

Cliff Hudder

Texas Review Press
Huntsville, Texas

FIRST EDITION, 2008

Requests for permission to reproduce material from this work should be sent to:

Permissions
Texas Review Press
English Department
Sam Houston State University
Huntsville, TX 77341-2146

ACKNOWLEDGMENTS:

Portions of this work appeared in *The Missouri Review*, Volume 22, Number 2 as the short story "The Equinox Wrapper," which received the Peden Prize in 2000.

The author is profoundly grateful to all of his friends and colleagues whose generous comments and encouragement helped throughout the writing of this work, most especially: Dave Parsons, Alicia Bankston, Therese Griffiths, Craig Livingston, Deanne Schlanger, and Mark Stelter. He is also also grateful for the support of writers and friends who have sustained him: Alan Ainsworth, Tony Diaz, Eddie Gallaher, Sharon Klander, Rich Levy, and Randy Watson. Finally, all he writes is influenced by the counsel of his teacher, Daniel Stern (1928–2007).

NOTE: *Splinterville*, while (at times) resembling a historical document, is a work of fiction. Names, places, incidents and characters are a product of the author's imagination or are used fictionally, and any resemblance to actual persons, living or dead, is entirely coincidental. This goes for the "editor" as well, and as for the comments in his prologue, his analysis, or any sources found in his footnotes, these the author would strongly advise against trusting at all.

Library of Congress Cataloging-in-Publication Data

Hudder, Cliff, 1957-
   Splinterville / Cliff Hudder. -- 1st ed.
      p. cm.
   ISBN-13: 978-1-933896-13-7 (pbk. : alk. paper)
   ISBN-10: 1-933896-13-2 (pbk. : alk. paper)
   1. Confederate States of America. Army. Texas Brigade--Fiction. 2. United States--History--Civil War, 1861-1865--Fiction. I. Title.
   PS3608.U3S65 2007
   813'.6--dc22
                                        2007042594

This book is dedicated to
Anne Wallace Hudder,
World's Best Mom,
and, always,
to Kazumi and Dylan

Splinterville

EDITOR'S PROLOGUE:

In fact, I was pondering how the Kernel of this whole Scene, was I to peel its shell, might have no Seed at all to its center.

Henry Oldham Wallace,
September 20, 1863

Post-structural theory, privileging as it does layers and contexts surrounding events over the "mere definition" of them, has taken over 140 years to catch up with Confederate infantryman Henry Wallace, and perhaps has much to learn from him yet. That his message is finally presented in this, the first widely distributed version of his odd and unwieldy letter, is somewhat remarkable, so various have been the circumstances working against its appearance before the public. Dealing with this material has allowed me in a direct manner to better comprehend Wartenweiler's idea of documentary history as not so much a record of past voices, but rather a "packaging of silences" by the power structures that determine which narratives are most acceptable. Private Wallace's silence would seem to have been packaged more securely than most, and, as editor, I applaud the publisher for bringing his story forward at last in this fine edition.[1]

I am aware that few besides specialists in this field and a small albeit vocal group of interested parties are even familiar with this peculiar document, the authenticity of which has been debated for decades. Its author remains an enigmatic figure who apparently did not survive the American Civil War. Although I have called this its first appearance, there is evidence of the letter's distribution in pamphlet form even before the South's surrender at Appomattox. One supposition is that its characterization of Confederate troops and their behavior at the enormous snowball fight in

---

[1] Jon K. Wartenweiler, *The Invisible History of Western Civilization* (New York: Livingston Press, 1994), 23.

Winter Quarters near Fredericksburg, Virginia, in January of 1863 met with such disapproval that each copy was hunted down by partisans and put to flames. To my knowledge, none of these earlier published versions remain in either private or library collections. Before the mid-twentieth century scholars knew the letter only by paraphrases within secondary sources. Problematically (especially for those who question its authenticity) no clear provenance exists for the text here presented, taken from what is purportedly the original handwritten letter itself, a document uncovered in 1963 in a "blind lot" at a Beaumont, Texas, antique auction by the late Professor Eric Hirschorn of Cisco University. That this document is in fact an elaborate hoax perpetrated by Dr. Hirschorn is a recent theory that has gained some prominence.[2]

Uncertainties remain. Still, after examining the "letter" in full, down on the floor, crawling at times, at other times aided by a powerful magnifying lens and strong flashlight, working day by day and month by month through the difficult passages, I could not help but gain the sense that I was experiencing the work, the words, and the heartfelt sentiment of a genuine personality—if not an insightful genius. That this was a forger's attempt to construct an individual psyche whole cloth became more and more untenable the more deeply I poured over the text (and I do mean poured *over*). Further research serves only to heighten this belief.

---

[2] For details as to the holograph's discovery, see Eric Hirschorn. "Our Business Here This Day': Infamous Civil War Letter Uncovered at Auction." *Western Histoircal Yearbook* 18 (Fall 1965), 84. The document is mentioned in Edwin Ainsworth's exhaustive investigation into the "Deadly Gap" exploited by Confederate troops during the Northen Georgia campaign: O*nly Following Orders: Thomas J. Wood and Rosecrans' Disaster*, (New York, Bugle Press, 1979), 54; as well as Adolph Mark Bell's "Psychotropics of the Civil War" *Military History of the Southwest*, (Spring 1976), 101. For the forgery theory, see Alan Colfatt, "Defending the Brigade: The Controversial 'Letter' of Henry O. Wallace." *Journal of the Center for Southeast Texas Studies*, (Fall 1995), 54-59.

It is the case that what little attention has been focused on this document inclines towards the contentious, and this should be addressed. I will venture to put forth that the controversies stem mainly from Private Wallace's membership in a unit which retains for many a strong emotional attachment, and which he himself calls "this Brigade of Renown." Hood's Texas Brigade was revered as "Robert E. Lee's shock troops," "The first in advance, the last in retreat," and so forth, and perceived critiques to the reputation of this unit are even today largely unwelcome, especially by those aforementioned interested parties. I, however, believe that thoughtful readers will find absolutely nothing in Wallace's missive that impugns Hood's Texas Brigade.[3]

As to the basics of presentation: the holograph of this document, dubbed by historians the "Chickamauga Letter" or "Equinox Wrapper" (hereafter referred to as the EW) and now in my possession, exists on a sheet of brown craftpaper twenty-four inches in width and an astonishing forty-one feet in length; hence, when Private Wallace speaks of writing on "hands and knees," this should not be reckoned metaphor. (As alluded to above, it was the same way I had to read it.) The hemp manila roll Private Wallace employed for his composition is of a type commonly utilized in the nineteenth century for packaging mailed parcels and grocery items. It is quite likely that Private Wallace found his "stationary" among the equipment hastily discarded by Union troops in their retreat from Northern Georgia. Needless to say, the paper is not of archival quality, and the letter survives now in a fragile state. Laboratory examination of fibers indicate

---

[3] My defense of the letter in a series of articles for the *Journal of the Center for Southeast Texas Studies* resulted in an avalanche of mail and email, of which the following could be considered representative: "Dear contrarian neohistorian hack set on glorification of any but red-blooded, heroic, Anglo ancestors for purposes of pursuing your own perverted self-interests: It is truly to be hoped that you do not die soon as it is doubtful you will have enough Indian, Mexican, jew [sic] or *other* friends around brave enough to carry your coffin . . . ." etc.

the parchment is of the correct era, but because the text was written in pencil rather than ink, ion-diffusion tests cannot determine when that paper was actually written upon. As I've pointed out elsewhere, this by itself is no strong argument for forgery.[4] For myself, I have little doubt the EW was composed without pause over the course of one evening and the following morning, September 20 and 21, 1863, on the field of conflict north of Snodgrass Hill, directly following that bloody encounter now referred to as the Battle of Chickamauga.

As judged from the hand-cancelled Confederate postmark and address on its reverse upper left corner, the paper roll was used as covering for a relatively small package mailed to Isaac Williamson at Bold Springs, Texas, in October of 1863. Creases and wear marks on the craftpaper, in addition to its great bulk, indicate that it must have been wound many times around what Dr. Aaron Dickinson has come to call the "mysterious parcel" or "interior of mystery." I believe, however, that any reader who took the trouble to unroll the text through to its conclusion would find a clear indication of the package's probable contents. After this wrapping, folds and crease marks indicate a rope or twine was used to tie off the roll at either end, no doubt giving the bundle the appearance of a very large, individually wrapped toffee. Whether the intended recipient, Mr. Williamson, received this package or read the involved communiqué scrawled on its interior is, like much concerning the EW, uncertain.

The text is here presented as nearly as possible to the form in which it was written, although, given its unusual configuration, particular emendations have been necessary for readability, and for display on a standard page. Spelling, save in the case of certain colloquialisms, has been made to conform to modern practice. Punctuation has been supplied where necessary in order to more clearly present the author's

---

[4] Jules DeRossier, "Heroic Misinterpretation: Alan Colflatt and the 'Equinox Wrapper'." *Journal of the Center for Southeast Texas Studies* 26 (Spring 1996), 274-76.

text. Underlined portions in the original appear as italicized. Some original passages were underlined two or three times, but indicating such has been deemed unnecessary to the presentation.

As mentioned, the holograph is written in pencil, and the script—faded in many places—was jotted down in a difficult to decipher, cursive scrawl at what appears to have been a fierce rate. Additional bleaching, smearing, and voids have made for difficulty in determining content, although original pencil scorings could on occasion be uncovered by patient examination with a flashlight held at an angle. Some portions of sentences are missing or simply cannot be worked out, but where possible are approximated in brackets. Quirky parentheticals and the use of ellipses all come from the author. His capitalization has not been altered, nor his frequent use of numerals, plural verbs with singular and collective nouns, non-standard articles, and so forth.

The name "Henry Wallace" (without any "O" or "Oldham") appears on muster rolls of L Company, 4th Regiment, Texas Brigade from its formation throughout the Georgia and Tennessee campaigns of 1863—although Dickson, Ulrich, and Colflatt point out correctly that the name does not appear on records at the time the unit disbanded at Appomattox Courthouse, April 9, 1865.[5] Private Wallace is otherwise unaccounted for in official correspondence as far as I can tell, and my assumption is that he met his end at Chattanooga, or possibly later, resisting the southern push of Grant's army through Virginia, a procession of carnage in which Hood's Brigade played an active and fatal role.

I would like to express my appreciation to the late Professor Eric Hirschhorn of Cisco University for allowing me access to the "Equinox Wrapper," as well as for his assistance during the final months of his life in preparing this unusual document for publication. I would also like

---

[5] Aaron Dickinson, William Urich and Alan Colflatt. *Tex-erfeit: Molding History to PC Myth in the Lone Star State.* (Washington on the Brazos: Barrington Press, 2001), 48-9.

to include my appreciation for all who have attacked the authenticity of Private Wallace's admittedly curious document. The EW has been accused of every sin common to historical forgery, including lack of provenance, erroneous information, internal inconsistencies, similarity to other suspected forgeries, and premature and anachronistic content. Investigating the letter for these attributes is a legitimate exercise. That after investigation it can be argued that these attributes apply to the document in question, however, has not been convincingly demonstrated. Nevertheless, as is often the case when dealing with the past, scholars are encountered who are worthy of great praise, not because their admonitions are correct, but because they significantly promote our knowledge of history as a result of being so completely mistaken.

For this, I salute them.

Jules H. DeRossier, May, 2005
Austin, Texas

Somewhere in Nth Georgia
September 20—

SIR:

I was there at the death of your dead boy Clinch and though I did not see his killing, me and your dead boy killed 2 days here in Nth Georgia, but your Clinch lived only 1 and 1 half days of it, him denouncing the while till he met his end and at the end he did not straggle. Your dead boy, a Man of Strong and Brave and True if sometimes mulish and unaccommodating character, this Clinch of yours is over. Neither hard travel nor diseases of winter has done it, Sir. No tree fell upon or crushed him, it is Death in Battle I describe and write now of to you.

On the 2nd of the 2 of our days upon this field I come upon our state's Major General John Bell Hood—he faced me around and spoke: —*Look about, Cog, that is my Machine you spin inside, see how much Equality you can find, how much Balance, you Speck, sir, you cannot Balance your Own Self, why can you not be more like your Companion the Vexatious Clinch?* I give him a Yes Sir, for I know he was correct, it was like he wrote [my] life on a grain. It was your dead boy, not me, who had the Brave Part of this campaign, I am nothing greater than the one who survived it, what this morning I took itself a Worthy Goal, yet I have Clinch to thank for that and wonder what story I might have to tell different had he not said what he did when we got off the trains. I have him to thank for bringing me through lead and ice (ice being worst) and for all this I am on hands and knees and also writing and sending this what little remains to.[6]

---

[6] Private Wallace's veneration of Hood (1831-1879) is characteristic of those who served under that officer, though history has not been kind to his war record. "Though an able soldier and leader at brigade level, as an administrator Hood lacked the most basic of skills, and as a strategist proved rash, impulsive, and inappropriately aggressive . . . . Confederate military history records no rout more thorough than that sustained by Hood at Franklin in 1864, resulting in the complete annihilation of the Army of Tennessee." Hood's Texas Brigade, of which Private Wallace

Reason we called your dead boy Clinch was when he saw something he wanted he would say—I am going to get that in my Clinches—I believe his name was Michael. This his Gathering Way was seen as troublesome activity but our Forces found your Clinch's far outreaching hands far outreached the best, sir, and soon all appreciated this, his Ardor. His stamp is on many men, and it might be said that though he will not return to you he did see a Large Part of the country, had Adventures and Trials and Many Experiences, and of every place he went he took a little Part of it with him. He was a Complete Soldier in all ways and shouldered his burdens with good humor, sometimes those what were not his too he would throw over a shoulder, but would take no ridicule and you should be proud as it would be easy for him to do so looking as he did uproarious. Your Clinch was smart and True and Brave and his paleness of flesh and obese aspect and the fact he come only to belly height on a normal man and his thick spectacles never kept him from being a complete package.

This is now our 2nd day in Nth Georgia—on our 1rst day our line went through wilderness and there was thousands of men in heavy bush and though the company is brought to small numbers I could not see the end of it nor far to any side. Mack was to the left side, Pard at the right, these being two others of your dear boy's companions, and one other of them, Ward, I do not know where he is tonight, then there was little Clinch 1 pace past Pard, draped in shrubberies to his bulb head. I did not see more than these 4 and some occasional other jacket or hat of our troop in a far direction, and every now and then a Enemy. I said to my companions this is a far from desirable dwelling place, yet they did not respond, as there hung a haze, ominous, what went over the scene with heavy weight and gloomed. Your Clinch scrutinized me through his lenses and told me I was

---

was a member, holds a number of records, many of these associated with the unit's "staggering casualty rate." See entry for "John Bell Hood," *The Confederate Encyclopedia*, (Chapel Hill, Freeland Press, 1979), 676-85. *passim.*

a man of Intellect for noticing the unpleasantness hereabouts and shot me the pod of his middle finger. This could lead you to believe that your dear dead boy and me was given to trading insults but this is not the case for I understood his insults all to be in the manner of fun and we never traded. He was of Good Nature, I have never known more good than inside your boy, but it was not always the case I recognized it. I did not know your boy at home as we lived far from Bold Springs, and what I could tell of him at first made me place him in that category of those to be stayed clear of yet I changed my tune.[7]

It came four in the afternoon by Pard's silver watch, then in comes our Enemy, clacking his guns like a boy with stick on piling, only faster than any boy with stick can clack, and yellow cloud drifted. Clinch said it was louder than two skeletons f—king on a tin roof you know how he talked. Me and Ward and Pard and Mack sighted rifles into the woods and Clinch crossed his arms and lowered his hat for he was not taken to shooting Enemies then nor doing anything much besides. Word come it was our own men ahead of us and we should not slaughter them, yet

---

[7] Colflatt writing in the *Journal of the Center for Southeast Texas Studies* (an entire essay responding to one of my letters to the editor) offers the opinion that many of the names in the EW are "just made up" and do not align with those found in official records of L Company, 4th Texas. "Ward," however, is well-represented in muster rolls, as well as state and county registries—see my note, page 13 of this edition. Furthermore, it is obvious that Private Wallace and his colleagues have a penchant for nicknames, making identifications difficult at times, but not impossible using contextual clues. For "Pard" see my note, page 15. "Mack's" identity is indeed "an object of mystery," but if we assume Wallace's appellations bear resemblance to original names, this could be "Anthony McLemore" found on muster roles of Company L all the way to Appomattox, and mentioned in official reports of every battle, making him one of "The 300"—that handful of soldiers who survived the war from start to finish in Hood's Texas Brigade. See: Jules DeRossier, "You're Welcome to Your Own Opinion, but Not Your Own Facts: Mystery, Distraction, and the Equinox Wrapper," *Journal of the Center for Southeast Texas Studies*, 27 (Spring 1997), 34.

the opinion come another way that that was the Enemy in fact, and we best slaughter him or face bad times. The noise kept up and come on, and there was truth in both gossips as we barely missed killing some Arkansans fleeing from out of there very fast. They run in that way they have, saying —Forget this place, there is no point, behind them come the ziggering noise. Rain started to rain but that was lead cutting leaf and peckering trunk, splinters floated on our hats, this was bad times. Some fires started and added smolder and in places I know it was dense and man to man, muzzle to muzzle, but at our place we only slaughtered 1 or 2 a time through the smoke of it that was how they come in like lost men. There was tamp rods struck in the trees overhead, the pups forgetting to take them out when they shot. Over us mockingbirds got in a [tangle not knowing(?)] where to go, two of them after each other with beak and claw such that Clinch said even the birds is so hateful here, yet he made only as if to take a nap to wait it out. It was no place for a nap but a place for a Fight, sir, but lonesome—it was like me and Ward and Pard and Mack and your still living Clinch was gone out in a group to some burning woods by ourselves to meet other fellows for a disagreement.

We stayed out in this way a hour in smoke and confusion and Childes come around—a man from our company—Childes come running in a wild dance, a St. Vitus sort I can not describe and he twisted as he come, it must have looked a impossible thing and surprised our Enemy as They did not kill him though I hear he has now lost that arm.[8] After that your now dead Clinch called and pointed

---

[8] Many of Dickinson, Colflatt, *et al's* misgivings about the EW are well taken. I cannot locate any "Childes" in Private Wallace's company, although Wallace expressly identifies him as being a member, and it seems an unlikely nickname. There were two soldiers with that surname in the brigade as a whole, over seven among the entirety of the Southern forces present. P. L. Keith in *Hood's Texas Brigade: Its Fame, Its Honor, Its Renown*, (New York, Splitlark, 1926), 301, lists Malcom V. *Childress* of Company L as "killed at Chickamauga" but gives no date and mentions no wounded arm.

with his balloon eyes back where we had come from as after
Childes come through we did not see another person and
so we shook back through brush and found our line it had
retreated without us in all the noise we did not know it. I tell
this to tell you your son's Courage and Loyalty, his Strong
Bravery in face of Danger his talent also to lay calm beside
Danger a while and consider it in a reasonable way, plus his
Talent for getting in some rest before making a move to act
in a Correct Manner and retreat in Proper Fashion. Your
Clinch was smart and True and brave and the looseness of
his pale flesh, the rotund aspect of him, his very low height
and the fact that since Jan. 29 he refused to fire his piece
never made him less the Man.[9]

Major General John Bell Hood was our brigadier at
Dumphries and with us in Eltham's and Fair Oaks and at
Malvern Hill—both Clinch and me together served together
this Great Man, we charged behind him at Gaines' Mill, and
many have followed him to make this a Brigade of Renown,
and many of these have died or took sick and died and there
was Coleman who a tree fell on him and he died.[10] And these

---

It is possible that Wallace is simply mangling or mis-remembering
that man's name.

[9] "Jan. 29" is the first reference to the Battle of Splinterville in the
EW. Because of his wounds, General Hood made no official report
of the part taken by his division at Chickamauga, and it is especially
difficult to locate Wallace's position on September 19. It is somewhere
in the heavily wooded area on the Confederate "far left."

[10] Although I have not given up on locating Coleman (and also
consider it possible that this is someone from another Company), I
find no record of this name associated with L Company, 4th Texas.
Colflatt lists this and various "inaccuracies" of the EW as evidence of
its fraudulent nature. See: Colflatt, "Defending the Brigade. . ." 129.
I have posited elsewhere what I consider a reasonable query: "Should
perfect concord with later established historical evidence be the
required standard for documents written in an informal manner?—or
would it not rather be that such perfect correspondence *should
more convincingly alert the researcher to the likelihood of fraud?*" See:
DeRossier, "Heroic Misinterpretation: Alan Colflatt and the 'Equinox
Wrapper'." 285.

men must be presented as those who prove and support the strength and courage of this Brigade though there are also plenty in that group who are also only of normal strength and courage or maybe a little above. Your now dead Clinch I place in the higher category as he was normal in no way. Clinch and me had served Hood but had not seen him in person a while and thought him off mending his wounds and not on that field, and when I did come up on the General I was in a state of impressionability—this was on the 2nd day and your Clinch already dead—and just how those stars of that officer's buttons shined, and the fall of sun at his light brown hair that [made him appear(?)] like Jesus and his beard was black also like that of Jesus's, up on his costly looking mare as he was, yet lounging against a tree like watching a parade though there was balls flying, he caused me to feel shame and this has made me promise to write to you of your boy and his importance.

I do not know if you are a little man, sir, but Clinch of course was (and would say of himself how he was shorter than a Pig's Kick), and on the night before our work here we made a cold dunk in creek water[11] to arm-pits but Clinch was of a size he could not ford this save for Ward and me passing him 1 to another at the deep middle though Clinch claimed we like to drown him worse this time than Louisiana. He snuffled on the far rocks and said: —My d—mned feet did not touch the bottom, no more than my nostrils disturbed the d—mned surface, and he berated. Ward is from Family and Property and Clinch would forever grieve him over this, and said on that occasion Ward was not getting his own head wet in that creek as he stood on his cash. Ward never made himself better than others, and now is missing, and lost his servant a while back, his own nigger he brought along being at that point dead and of no service to him. Clinch asked Ward at the time of our first drawing script if this was for him a new experience, to what Ward asked if he meant holding money? and Clinch said

---

[11] Chickamauga Creek, forded by Longstreet's Division on the evening of September 18.

—No to hold it what was earned. Ward grinned at all this as well as the crack about standing on a pile in the Creek and passed your now dead boy along to Mack and myself like has was a sack of dirt, and tonight Ward is missing and I believe him dead.[12] Around us at that time on the other side of the creek was the leavings of Conflict—corpses strode in stances of surprise as no doubt some advance had forced the place. The Final Save One Night of Clinch's life come around and we did not know what was coming, but your Clinch went out to count 8 Enemy carcasses on the black rocks—none of them had shoes—plus a horse also killed, as adding up these remnants had become his habit. Your dear boy he always [included in his count(?)] horses and any other dead thing what might have got insensibly caught in way of harm, once there was a cow. He told me when he counted up more of Theirs than Ours it give him a kind of good feeling, and when he counted up more of Ours than Theirs it give him a bad kind, but otherwise he had stopped working up feelings but to wonder should he put the shot horses and creatures like that Exploded Cow on either side's count or [put them on(?)] some other list.

Your boy was not a boy I knew of from youth and in fact first heard of only as many talked of him after we left Texas, after we got to Louisiana and the passage through that state, as there was many swamps and low passages he had to be carried over. It was 10 days and 500 miles of water, mud, rain, and water.[13] I never spoke to your boy till we got off

---

[12] The best documented soldier in the EW, Arthur Love Ward was born in Tennessee, the son of Judge John M. Ward who moved his family to Montgomery County, Texas, in 1846. 1850 tax records show the judge's extensive landholdings were close to the community of Kentucky Landing, Texas, but he had a dwelling in the nearby town of Montgomery where it can still be seen during seasonal Yule-Tide home tours. Other family members included wife Susan Ann and Arthur's brother William Love Ward. Muster Roll, Company "L," Fourth Texas Infantry Regiment, dated September 16, 1861 (Confederate Collection, National Archives, Washington, D.C.).

[13] It is, by my reckoning, closer to two hundred miles.

the train at New Orleans, it is funny how a man can be in a same county and in fact a same army as another and not know him.

And we stayed together from that time to this morning, and looked after each other, that is why it is up to me to tell you of his demise, although fact is he mostly did the looking after and myself the getting took care of, and I am in a worry yet over what might happen to me now without him. Just on yesterday morning Clinch snuck a jar of brandy between us, only for him and my self, this jar he got off a corpse in the night as he had gone a scavenger, and this was a thing that he would do always, bringing back to me the best of his loot for a share, although this jar this time, sir, was a liquor of a Poisonous Kind, possibly planted by our ungenerous Enemy in enticing jars to cloud our reasons, and it could not be called tasty but as it was clear we had a large work ahead and I for one needing a boost of graceful spirit, I had some from that jar.

And this morning I woke up bone chilled, nostrils in wet leaves, suffering chatters and ready for fortifying, so me and Clinch tasted freely again from the jar—it possibly had turned a bit, but was tolerable. Also Clinch got some handfulls of mushrooms in the night—what he called bark tripes—these scraped off a dead trunk, and these gummy knobs was almost tasteless but that made up for what taste they did have what was odious. I do not know if they knew we were there, I do not know if they knew we had even arrived to fight, there never was breakfast, there never was stores for dinner, this was our 2nd day in Nth Georgia, the last of your boy's life, and we was hundreds of us near starved.[14]

---

[14] That the Texas Brigade was even in North Georgia for the battle of Chickamauga is a story of a mammoth logistical shift labeled by the Confederate high command as "Operational Plan Westward Ho," a fast, secret movement designed to deliver a surprise blow against Rosecrans' forces. On their move from Bowling Green, Virginia, to Catoosa Station, Georgia, the Texas Brigade traveled nine hundred miles, used eight different railroads, two sizes of track gauge, and negotiated eight major transfer points. Taking nine days for the entire

We raised up and come on, all brush and limb and thickness tramped under, and Clinch loaded his piece what made me think it was to be a special day for his rifle had not tasted powder since Jan 29.[15] The morning was cold but clear, while light touched the top of this forest. It looked wild and eccentric there, all the limbs was nitched, scorched, and stripped from the day before, there was yet smolder, and soon we come on a place where there was a corpse for every tree, a tree for every corpse, such that Clinch could not begin to count, these being perhaps some we had slaughtered the day before. After a quarter hour of our company creeping so and thrashing, Clinch and me started to yawn—this was because of the brandy—to where Pard says, What has all this death about got you bored?—and Clinch says, Well, it is getting old but not so old as you you broke up fossil. Pard is 42, has family and a piece of land, and so got the hard end of Clinch many times as being a crooked and Ancient Patriarch who creaked in the bones and it was rumored f-rted dust. This was all in fun and your boy's manner of friendliness. Old Pard's shirt was but scraps on him like the rest of us but his worst was the soles of his footwear, both had near flappered off—we have walked a fair way, sir, with Louisiana only the beginning—and that of his flapping boots, said Clinch, was just as well as Pard was anyhow too dense to drain p-ss from them was the instructions writ on the heels you know how he spoke.[16]

---

journey, the operation was indeed fairly "fast," but turned out to be not at all "secret." United States War Department, *The War of the Rebellion: Official Records of the Union and Confederate Armies* (Washington, Government Printing Office, 1880-1901) Series I. Vol 29, Part II, p. 706. Further reference to this source will be shown as "O.R.A." followed by the Series, Volume and page.

[15] Second reference to the Battle of Splinterville in the EW.

[16] Montgomery County, Texas, Courthouse records cast an ambiguous glow on "Pard" without fully illuminating him. Taking into account the advanced age at enlistment of the man described in the EW, his landowner status, and the fact that he was still alive after Chickamauga in 1863—still leaves this researcher with two potential "Pard"s. Esau Brace Harold is one—forty-four years old in 1863.

Clinch and me ate more of the mushrooms and had 2 more secret swallows of brandy, and this liquor made quick effect on our empty stomachs and heads, too, sir, as I soon lost the position of the sun among the trees and somehow developed a doubt as to whether we tramped into a fight or if we had not turned around, retreating to the trains to fight somewhere else some other time. As for your dead boy, he could gather no interest in any of it and just said, I, for 1, Henry, am in a foul and ponderous mood—this being when I believe he started to know what was coming, he become so grave and low—he said: What I say is this: That I am busying myself thinking about Mind.

—Mind?

—Mind, he said—About the hardness it can create for a man, plus also its capacity for working up discomfort over that what has but little chance of happening . . . and such.

—As for me, I said, trying to change the subject from these words what was uncharacteristic of him insofar as their complexity and moderate tone, —As for me I am noticing something peculiar about the corpses hereabouts—as I was.

Do you know, sir, in a room of pitch blackness, how if a man looks hard to make his eyes used to it he sees there are yet areas pitcher and blacker than others? Such that it is not the pitchness nor blackness he sees at all in some of those spots, but more a breed of light? Only light what

---

He returned to the county after the war but removed soon to farm in McLaren, serving there as a justice of the peace before his death in 1873. Farmer Evan Joshua Parr is a much more enticing possibility: forty-eight at the time of Chickamauga, died at the Battle of the Wilderness, May 7, 1864, and presumed buried in the common grave on that field. While Harold is closer in age to Wallace's claim, obvious reasons make "Parr" an attractive candidate for "Pard." Although the recruiting age for Confederate soldiers was 17-35, several in Hood's brigade were younger or older, including A. L. Banks of Company M, First Texas, who at fifty-six passed away on the march—his official cause of death listed as "old age." Stanley G. Ramsey, *Lee's Grenadier Guards: A Day-by-Day Sourcebook of Hood's Texas Brigade.* (Shelbyville, Angelina Press, 1934), 532.

shows something so uncertain he cannot know for certain what it shows at all?

Sir, this morning under those trees it was that way with those dead, they vibrated in a Uncertainty what rose and fell like waves of the Gulf—that being what I had not seen or experienced before riding on the steamer from Beaumont to Louisiana—the ride in the steamer from Galveston a marked occasion for them like me what had never even seen such a boat or been on open sea.[17] Among the trees and brush, the corpses glowing around us and blurring in waves what near made me have to stop completely and sit down, we come across 1 of the corpses, he had on the blue trousers of the Enemy but not much more, he was still moving and there was a buzz coming out of him, it was his tongue asking for water, and Clinch stopped to give him a taste of the brandy. Clinch wiped his own brow with his rag sleeve and said in his squeak voice—Jesus but there's so many, seems they had no room to die flat out, and I become overwhelmed by a sense of barrenness, of there being no point then even of unstopping that jar, nothing was to come of it, that even to stand up had no value. I had come too far since that steamer ride that the wavering land put me in mind of, and that ride by itself now seemed *too far*, and I was turning low and feeling beyond hope.

And it was because of this steamer and what your boy and my dearest friend took off it that I had first heard of Clinch, though there had been rumors too about a turkey gone from Governor Kay's place when we marched through it, plus stores of sugar missing at Camp Van Dorn and a whole suttler's place ransacked of goods of an evening in the summer in Houston City at that same camp, it was not till our wade across Louisiana that I come to connect *all* these incidents with Clinch. This hike through the swamps was a terrible [slog(?)] of a trip and one I will not forget, not least for meeting your Clinch at the end of it, for it was truly not until Brashear city and the ride that near rattled our bones and what was left of the tatters of us that Clinch come up

---

[17] The steamer *Florilda* almost certainly.

and made a comment on my shoes what has kept with me always and what thinking about even now drives the blade of sadness in.[18]

And so we remained as companions from that time until this morning crossing that forest so scorched and filled with death, for as he give a sip to that Enemy I could see what Clinch said of those corpses was true, this place of thicket was next to filled up with them, all Outlandish and Vibrating (if you looked close you could see fine hairs growing on the backs of the arms of them, dirt set in the cracks of their cheeks), most every 1 was propped against or turned over another 1. The Enemy Clinch give the sip to gagged and said, —*Gawd* —*Gawd, I asked for water*, and so Clinch said, —I only got this, son, sorry—what was how your boy would talk to another man who was wounded, this one's chest all cracked and bloodied, his face grey with spots blooming—any man with a Grievous Wound and spread flat, Clinch would tend to talk to as a child and not so much a Enemy. I yawned more and a warm tickle started at my eartips, the Company was thrashing, leaving us to straggle, and those corpses and trees trembled in the morning, maybe caused by leaves rustling. There was not much of Clinch sticking above the brush save his rotund head and spectacles, and he looked flush-cheeked and sad.

And I have said how at the end your Clinch he did not straggle although in fact right *up* to the end he did, it being his Common Practice to do so, but this is not to Cast Blame so much as to say it was what come to be expected of him—Clinch, sir, being given more slack to wander, to hold and poke around especially by our 1rst 2 Captains—a kind of freedom I also gained for being at his side and helping,

---

[18] Company L left Montgomery, Texas, on July 25, 1861, lodged overnight on the grounds of planter "Governor" Walter M. Kay's plantation while on the march, and formed a few days later at Camp Van Dorn in Harrisburg, spending less than one month there in training. See Muster Roll, Company "L," Fourth Texas. Wallace never mentions what went missing from the steamer *Florilda*, presumably appropriated by the acquisitive Michael "Clinch" Williamson.

but that was not always the case and I guess now will not be the case again. This is to say that your Clinch was something more of scout than soldier—though deadly of aim when he chose to lift his piece—it come about because of you, sir, the truth being it was a story about you yourself what caused him to change to this role of free scout from his previous one what was bound prisoner.

Clinch become of such importance on our march and it is a importance I have yet to make clear in this my account of him as to how he fit with our Company of Renown. I believe in addition to this windy they told of you—and it occurs to me now you may not even have heard this tale and it might be a stretcher—his Great Position come because of all we could not bring when we started across Louisiana. Mostly the sick and many supplies, we had to leave these at Coles as some officer had not arranged enough wagons nor mules—and if we had known the nature of the place we were to enter I believe we would have jumped off at Coles forever, yet we were untried then and did not know, but as for the windy:[19]

It is a story I heard (about yourself, sir) in our tramp after getting off the steamer and heading into the troublesome swamps, and of the days we spent in the swamps they were made further unpleasant by having only one among them without rain, so we had the dampness coming at us both ways. Our first day after getting off the steamer was a rainy march through muck and where we stopped wasn't far because we had to unload what we had to send back for the rest—left at Coles—and these arrived at close of day on the few wagons, the sick spread on them, plus also one boy more captive than patient as he had got in trouble (this being your Clinch, sir), and he rode with feet dangled off the end of the last wagon, wrists bound though

---

[19] "Coles" is Coles Station, a short march from the *Florilda's* unloading point at Niblett's Bluff on the Sabine River. Stanley Ramsey describes the same transportation problem from the viewpoint of Company "H." *From Here to Defeat*, (Beaumont, Texican Press, 1979), 31.

he did not seem to mind but only glad not to be walking in that awesome mud. So that was how he started out with our Company, as a mysterious figure bound and tied and unruly like a wild creature.

We cooked and had some rainy coffee and it was Ward said he knew that boy and his family at Bold Springs, and they was a Famous Group and Ward's nigger kept cursing the rain but Donovan said he knew of them Williamsons, too (and here, sir, he was referring to your family).[20] I was keeping myself close to Ward in those days on advice of my Mother, him being someone I should associate myself with by her lights. Ward told this story, sir, what I pass to you as it may well be created out of lies but you should hear it in that case, too, although I have no mind to set you against Ward or his Family for it, it being a tale speaking more to your Sincerity of Purpose, Thrift and Cleverness of Mind than any other matter. For myself it was only days before I would myself stick so close to Clinch and stay that way until the very time of his death what was today, and have little truck with Ward after that although I am hoping he is not dead like your boy Clinch.

I have a terrible headache and there is a stench here that is terrible, but I press on, for Ward said that Strange Boy up there on that wagon was the sire[21] of the Williamson at Bold Springs on the Upper Coushatta, a man who had a particular trait or habit of mind when it come to his possessions. Ward's own father Judge Ward had told him this Williamson always wanted his possessions to be in plain view. It was such that he (meaning *you*, sir) could not *bear* to leave these his treasures out of his sight, and if this was from having a wife who went out on him Ward was not sure, for this Mrs. Williamson woman one day told her husband [eight or nine

---

[20] Donovan A. Clinton of Grimes County, Texas. Muster Roll, Company "L." No information from the 1850 Census. This seems one of the few times Private Wallace actually calls someone by his first name.

[21] Most likely the educated Arthur Ward (Transylvania College, Lexington, Kentucky) said "scion"—offspring or descendant.

words—indecipherable] and then left forever, but Ward did know this Man kept a Close Compound in Bold Springs where all he owned could be held near, and he kept his boys at home without letting them much wander, feeling, as he did, the world had no great offerings to add to what Bold Springs offered already. —It is for this reason, said Ward, —I am surprised to see this boy here but not surprised to see him troublesome— and it was true about the trouble part as our 1rst Captain was already finding him a handful.[22]

It was the case, said Ward, this man Williamson (yourself, sir) like any Man, found it a necessity to go to Montgomery Town for salt and other requirements from

---

[22] Montgomery County Census of 1850 lists the household of Isaac Bonham Williamson (birthplace Georgia) and Mary Williamson (Arkansas) along with five sons all born in Texas: Sam Houston, John A., James Edward, Richard W., and Michael H. The family does not appear on tax records, nor do they reappear in later census reports. Colflatt et. al. point strongly here towards terms like "1rst Captain" and the later mentioned "2nd" and even "3rd Captain," as evidence that the EW is in fact the product of no Confederate soldier of the nineteenth century. While the chain of command in the Army of Virginia commonly included 1rst, 2nd, and even the now defunct 3rd *Lieutenants*—(each in charge of a "platoon,")—there would be only *one* Captain elected to lead each company of soldiers (Colflatt, "Defending the Brigade." 219). My response then and now is that no private—no forger for that matter—would misapprehend the basic Company level chain of command in such a manner, causing me to seek another reason why these terms might be used by Private Wallace. The answer turns out to be so superficially obvious that it had to be pointed out to me by my thirteen-year-old son, and has to do with the way Wallace uses numerals rather than spelling out numbers of any kind. Company L had already lost two Captains by the time of Chickamauga. Obviously "1rst Captain" refers to the man they left Montgomery, Texas, with in 1861, Captain Rudolph Perry, killed at Gaines Mill in 1862. The "2nd Captain" is the man who took his place, Lewis R. Moore, who will play a gallant role in the EW's account of the Battle of Splinterville, but be killed assaulting Little Round Top at Gettysburg in 1863. By the time of Chickamauga, Company L is on its third ("3rd") commander, James G. Shaw. DeRossier, "You're Welcome to Your Own Opinion," 37.

time to time and procure such provender as even the Eden of Bold Springs did not provide. (And Ward did describe this community of Bold Springs as —*A lower place on the Upper Coushatta*, and a locale of shacks and green swamp but I have never been up there, sir, although to hear your Boy tell, this did not seem the case for rather he did go on about how good Bold Springs is, sir, he was awful high on Bold Springs, and spoke most only about his desire to return to it, to get away from all war and cold especially cold.) Although this Father, then, he could take his boys with him to town, and even feel his house and grounds safe with the many vicious dogs he kept to watch over all, he worried over some wagons he had, as there were two of these, fine possessions, though he had only the one horse for pulling what meant he would have to leave one or other wagon at his home, the horse being too lamed to pull nearly one.

This Old Man, then, the Williamson Patriarch (being you according to this story), he found hisself with but one way out, [according to] the now Lost Ward, when it come to looking after the both of the wagons—it being the only possibility for him now his woman had left and her able, it was said, to place a bullet in the ear of a man at a hundred yards, a rifle wizard and no doubt part of the reason Clinch had such Deadly Aim despite the need for specs. This Sole Solution was for him to take Both Wagons to Montgomery Town at once, driving ahead with the first till he could but barely still make out the one behind, then unhitching and riding his animal to get hitched again to the one left back and hauling that second past the first in a kind of leapfrog fashion until only so far as that *first* could yet be seen—the boys in part helping once they was of age with the hitching and the unhitching and the keeping watch behind. I believe Ward found this a odd and funny enterprise, as it tickled him so to tell it (as such men will be tickled, sir, what have so much they need never keep a eye on any of it), and it is a fact our 1rst Captain listened to this tale and had seen the wagons come in that night with the sick laid flat but little round Clinch dangling his feet out the back of one of them, tied up to keep him from appropriating from the

Louisianians more than they knew they give, and it could be our 1rst Captain had a type of Revelation concerning the way Clinch's troublesomeness could be made to serve, or maybe he had another kind of Vision what shivered him and give him Terrors—of having to be like Clinch's own father (yourself, sir), and going along in this come-along fashion all the way to Richmond, Virginia, and I believe that as more rain come on him that night he got resolved and decided to approach Clinch the next morning.

I say it because it was that next day what was the one out of all when there was no rain, and one in which we did not move from where we camped for this was when the 1rst Captain put all at ease to dry in the sun—and it was to be the last of the sun we'd see, sir, until New Orleans—for we was to enter into 8 days of swamp and slog what would fair disintegrate all those fine supplies we stacked and ordered at that crossroads—and all rested and dried save a select band your own Clinch included who was set on the neighborhood to seek transportation, and it sounded too like our 1rst Captain had got less squeamish on how such should be found, only that *found it should be*, and by that evening there was a set of wagons for us to ride, also carriages, two fine springless hacks, down to carts and some others what looked mere barrows, it was a collection, plus the gangliest and unruliest of animals to haul them. We loaded these vehicles high the next day and got aboard as the rain started peckering down and I did think the finest there was the Springless Hack and your now dead boy holding the reigns of it though I heard later on he did not much think of it as special. I did not ride with him nor near him on our long spread out trail, yet learned well from others how this short man said the hack was nothing compared to the quality of those owned by his Father at Bold Springs, and Ward said when he heard it he had to bite down.

Irregular cloud bursts come through those days what give a sort of relief from the steady drizzle, and the 1rst Captain drew out a line for us to New Orleans but he must never have traveled it before—I cannot remember this man's name now but feel him a well-meaning although not able sort[23]—for my belief is he had by ill luck discovered the wettest and most miserablest route to that place out of all others, yet from that day Clinch ceased being a trouble for him, instead becoming a Talent, and every day Clinch and a few others scattered ahead or lagged behind and brought in more transport also food and coffee.

At the Cowcashew[24] come another incident what I would not include about save it so concerns your boy, it being a place we crossed in a Schooner fine and dry, but at its Eastern side there stood a rising bank high and by this time muddy and marsh-like besides, also slick, and though I still did not know him only hearing about him your Clinch's fame was grown among us. This day was one of the most arduous not of this War so far but of this Life so far, as there was a Great Feat of ropes and pulling to gain high ground with those wagons, and by the end of it, all felt reduced. Lines was tied to the tongues of coaches and burrows and a company of men a time would haul slow at the ends of these to raise each and the rain fell, soaking all. Then there come a sort of accident there being a large grey buggy of uncommon weight what joined this uphill parade—such that even when it got emptied off and the contents marched up that hill on our backs it was Brute Dismay pulling it over the rise. I was at marching and carrying and slogging up this steep wet place with a sack when this fancy buggy give loose—it had made it already near the top of the bank—and the screams come *Lookout!* so I throwed myself with my parcel and got covered in mud but it did not matter as I was yet covered already, just in time to see it—the buggy—come in a long caroom, jostling and leaping and never staying with all four wheels in mud, it rolled. I feared it was to burst or overturn to kill a man, it kept coming, the strain too high, I suppose, for those above, all letting go at once. It slid past me in a terrible rattle but then I heard more coming there was a

---

[23] Rudolph Perry. More evidence that Private Wallace actually knows what he's talking about but is merely terrible with names. The brigade roughly followed the path of present-day Interstate 10.

[24] Calcasieu River.

sound of —*Aaaaaaaaaaaarrrrrrrr*, for so at the end of the hemp behind it there was a man, him having been in the final or anchor spot with this line wrapped in some way or caught up on his arm that he could not loosen when others stepped aside. He come splayed with his long holler and wail, his heels dug in so they shot mud over him in a sheet, and from time to time it seemed he would be driven down in that muck like a stake, the spray of it come and covering up his glasses, too, him blinded, sir, it was your Clinch again. Him riding and hauling and gobbling mud after that buggy, being unsuccessful at all alone stopping it, and rolling a bit with the effort, and by the time of the bottom he was under near layers of this trail filth, and had tore a swash down that road to make it impassable what he had done just with his body mostly heels. The 1rst Captain give him a good riding down as well what I could hear up the bank, and asked did he mind to take with him Everything out of the Louisian, dirt and filth as well?—and the rain poured, and I heard later that your boy replied he had no need of that filth as the filth of Bold Springs was of a better quality, as fine as that found any place on earth and finer than most.

And it is hard to describe if you have not done so, sir, how being a part of a Large Group under Stress delivers a aspect of truth to the saying that such a company becomes *Forged under Fire* and starts to take on in common what in a individual would be described a personality, and fact is your boy was the proper instrument in the forging of that what our company showed, the personality of Company L, and though I still had not said a word to him I started to feel I knew something of him, that he was part of my Own Existence as there did not pass a hour in the next days I did not hear his name or some New Exploit assigned him, or heard some saying coming out of the members of that company what found its source at your own boy's strong influence. This is a strange yet true fact what could be also from the dire circumstance we found ourselves in soon for as we left the mud and the rain we traveled next in a country of swamp and rain, sometimes over ankles the black muck of it, sometimes over waist. The discomfort of having lakes of black water to walk on and hard drops to walk under was accompanied by a further disadvantage being mosquitoes what plagued and come in billions, causing us to march to the music of slaps and curses every step until there arose a new kind of game what lasted at least four more days to New Iberia—this being started I believe by Mack although for that matter it could have been Ward's nigger as he was a clever one (he is now dead) who would join in with some of the best. This game we were into was in its whole nothing to describe and nothing now what would strike a man as a strong amusement save was he there to share the awesome fun of it, but what I am saying is that not a event no matter how small could occur about the conditions of our march, nor statement made—such, for example, that it sure was *mighty wet* or the like—that another person would not up and become disagreeable saying—No this is not Wet you should see the Wetness of Bold Springs, and then cause another to pipe in that—The Water There—meaning at your's and Clinch's home community—The Bold Springs Water was of such a Wetness as to make *this* water *Quite Parched* by comparing, and then it would go on in that way and gather more steam, such that, yet, —The *Dryness* there, too, (that of Bold Springs), was really Something to Behold, being that there was no sort of dryness nowhere else quite so dry as it and, in fact, though there might be some among us who thought we could have at one time or point been in what might be called by common man Arid Circumstances we were, in fact, Only Disillusioned, compared with the dryness of Bold Springs and, in fact, said the 1rst Captain (who had caught up the knack of it), we had probably actually at the time been suffering under a *Species of Merely Reduced Dampness Without Knowing* we being too indiscriminate to recognize such as being moist when laid aside a good dry Bold Springs day. Certain, to give Louisiana its due, the mosquitoes there were vicious in temperament, yet at Bold Springs the Vulture Sized Blood-Suckers come armed with knives and clubs, and did they fail to suck all your juices (it was Donovan put this one in)—to get your blood from you they'd take you to the Courthouse with a

Lien on the rest, and yes, these Louisiana skeeters might be large but a least they did not Crawl in the Bed with you nor Hog the Covers as them Bold Springs kind did, nor Throw their Legs over you in a friendly way once they was comfortable and warm. Your boy Clinch would hear these meandering statements what grew and he would smile in a small way about half way through some, and get kind of steamed at others, and this just brought out the company with more of the same, till your Clinch had to let loose with a confrontational jeer against the whole of them and their families also and saying finally such statements as—I met you now two months past and must say I have been the same ever since—or—I had used to hold you all beneath my contempt but now have changed my mind, and the like, all in his high screak voice.

We slogged in this horrid yet near crazed manner for tortured miles each like the last till finally conditions began to take a turn for the worse, and we entered what the 1rst Captain's map called the *Grand Marias* but what we all come to label quick *The Great Miry*. And now the rain *did* start to fall, sir, and made our hats draggy and sad, and these were most the only parts of us above water for it got very Deep in this section so at least the mosquitoes got a reduced fare and did not much bother us except for cheeks and noses and foreheads and ears and lips and necks, although maybe they laid off because the alligators was having too big a time bothering us themselves. Nobody got bit by one but they did slide around so in the grasses and every time I felt a brush of root or stick in the wet murk I thought it was a gator planning to get a taste and my stomach went Very Loose. I came eye to eye with two of them and maybe they feared our numbers or took it to heart when both Pard and another man speared one each with their bayonets and held him overhead to show his kin.[25] Such trekking continued on

---

[25] Many extant letters and reminiscences from soldiers who traveled from Texas to Richmond, Virginia, in 1861 mention the terrible conditions of the march between Niblett's Bluff and New Orleans. Perhaps the best known comes from the Reverend David Zimmermann.

in a worsening fashion for a few more days till we reached a river and marched up the bank of that a while dealing only with rain and no food and the falling apart of our fine uniforms with the blue trim the county spent so much on, as they—the uniforms—all started disappearing from view and leaving us somewhat stark, still it was pretty much a improvement in circumstances. When some other wagons come along of New Iberia to pick us up they almost did not want to as we was wet and naked half starved specimens, sir, but they fixed us and fed us up as they could and took us to Brashear City for the train. What we had that did not come apart or ruin in the wet we pretty much dropped off as being too heavy to mess with, we did not have coats, and many Texas heroes was without trousers when they got into the cars for the hardest jostle of their lives what shook apart everything we had left and caused the clear demise of more than one man. Pard's watch—what is from England and a Miracle of Mechanical Construction as it survived that damp walk and even that train ride and clacks on to this day—this watch told us it was midnight plus two minutes when we come to a stop at New Orleans and it is the truth that at that point I first made acquaintance of your son and boy, at that moment of getting off the car—I believe it was one designed to travel with cows—and I felt myself, sir, at the burned off edge of the world. Lanterns on a walkway showed only a sliver's worth of light and I near poured around in that car, sir, finally just coming to sit and hang my legs off a while, I was not sure I could even get down my strength was poor. I watched my companions stagger off and watched their backs a while—a sight, as I say, I was to see often once I partnered with your Clinch as he did not walk

---

See *My Time with Hood's Brigade* (San Antonio, Hill Country Press, 1960), 30–31. Private Anthony Fuller from Company E reported in a letter to his sister reproduced in his hometown newspaper that this part of the trip included "an expanse of ground so quagmiry buzzards will not fly over in fear their shadows will bog." *The Coastal Telegraph* (Rockport), August 19, 1861. Corroborative accounts from such widely differing sources further convince me of the EW's authenticity.

quick on them little legs and favored the rear part of any formation for his scouting—and I dropped what was left of my shoes down on the gravel as I had removed these during our jostle on the train—I was getting more heel blisters from the back and forth racking of that car than I did ever from walking through Louisiana, and the edges of that car did collide so against the skin and bone—and I thought I was alone, the last straggler, but come to find some other figure appeared—a mound of pure rag and tore flannel come rustling from a far dark corner off a pile of rope, scrabbling low on all fours like a creature to where I was, and looked near dead himself right then though he had yet two more years of life left in him (and there is a lesson, there, sir about his Resilience) . . . but he showed the effects from all the mud and rain and exposing, his pants was no more, he had but pulled the ruins of his shirt as far down over his underjohns as he could, he smelled a bit, sir. A powerful aroma rose off him and assailed, it was your Clinch, sir, and I at that moment did not want anything to do with him, myself still considering him no matter how entertaining still of a type My Mother had put me in warning sure against (for such were my thoughts at that time), and a Bad Influence, prone to telling tales and insults, a drinker of Spirits—for so he was held to be—when the occasion permitted, a borrower of whatever was not screwed down solid plus nailed. In later days I come to know these unpleasant rumored aspects of him to be the case but they did not matter, yet right then I moved from him as he scooted up, but he did not ask for help or for a hand in getting down, only clung his head off over the side and kind of panted like crawling off them ropes took his Final Powers. A breeze what was also wet come from somewhere and the eaves of this depot dripped rain, and he looked off to the ground and said —What is that?—all in a way of surprise such that I could not much tell was he even asking something or was it more just a statement near of alarm, and before I remembered how I had promised myself and My Mother I would not speak to such types even when the occasion permitted I said —What's *what?* And he seemed overcome to notice me even being there, though I had been there from the 1rst, and he said *That Down There* and I could tell, then, by the motions of his unusual eyes what he was talking about—and I looked and I told him that was my *shoes* and he shook his head. —Your *shoes!* And I said that they were (for I had saved a little foot leather after that long slog and though they did not look like much I could not see them insulted in any way and that was what I expected this heap of rags to come out with, some kind of commentary as to their state of decay), but he said, like amazed —That is a *very* lucky thing, ain't it?

And had I not asked that what I did next of your boy him and me might have remained strangers a good while (though I do not doubt we would have become companions eventually, sir) for I felt like only moving on and finding a place to drop and sleep. I felt like I was at some far station with the next stop for me some other existence, but I did not climb down just then, I did not put on them shoes and walk, but asked, —It is a very lucky thing *why?*—and he said —It is a very lucky thing we stopped so close to 'em, and I cannot describe it otherwise than this, sir, that at that time my heart went to him, and so I did step down in them shoes and did help your boy Michael Williamson off that train and we ended together that night on a cotton bale in a warehouse, spread out on it soft like it was a cloud though there was stiff ropes across parts of it, it did not matter, we was far from home.[26]

And so we remained as companions from that time until this morning crossing that scorchy and death-filled forest so filled with death, and on this day, standing in this

---

[26] While Private Wallace does not record it, Company L and five other companies continued on a twelve hundred mile train ride to Richmond, Virginia, arriving September 12, 1861, utilizing one-seventh of the railroad mileage then in the Confederacy. They had been on the road approximately sixty days since leaving Montgomery, and traveled 1,800 miles, over two hundred on foot. Shawn F. Payne, *The Confederate Railroad*, (New York, Blinn Press, 1950) Map insert back cover. Merlin S. Taylor, *Defeat at the Depot* (Carbondale, Illinois College, 1951), 147.

thicket as all our troops went wallowing from us as they had the night we got to New Orleans, Clinch was looking hard at all the death and pondering out loud what made it peculiar compared to all the everyday death we met with every day—and I said I did not think it was all that different, maybe just a little more shimmery sort, but good and dead the same, and he said there was yet something about these corpses unusual, although he could not put his finger on it. He examined the poor wounded enemy some more, then looked some more at the already dead around and then —NO! he said and snapped his fingers. —What it is, Henry, is that the face of a man's murderer gets etched on the eyes of him what's killed, and there is *so much murder here*, that is what we are seeing as peculiar: all of these other murder eyes looking back at us through these dead men like a mirror show.

Clinch's own eye-bulbs was so huge I was disoriented —That is a wife's tale, I put in. And Clinch said, —It is the case, and the Enemy with the Grievous Wound said, —*Gawd kill me or get me water you are ugly as a troll.* —And you, said Clinch, have a face reminiscent of a barrel of pickled a—holes, to what the Enemy seemed to possess no quick response. —Yet fact is, said Clinch, we are not supposed to make a racket or waste a cartridge, and he turns to me, —But if we did, if we shot him, it would be us, he says, —You and me Henry, etched in his eyes as those last beings he sees, his murderers . . . and then we could check it out.

And I did not mention it but felt it a awful negative way to approach a morning and I felt so low besides, and— though I also did not say it because of Clinch's mood—why did he have to use that word and keep doing it so? It did not even occur to me to think of it that way before, so it was your dead boy Clinch first put that idea in my mind, that idea of Murder, sir, and the Enemy said —*Gawd, will you four midgets stop talking and shoot me or let me drink?*

—I am no midget, says I, —And there are but two of us.

—Though we could stab at you, said Clinch, if you wanted it—and I did not want to have to do it, I did not want to have to go after this man, he was naught but a tongue, he was nothing but a voice so far away—but we did not have to as the Enemy cracked one eye apart, it looked up at us 1 to the other it was all bloodshot, he said —I guess not.

I'll prove it anyhow! says your boy, and he takes us off from the dying man to scuttle and examine some of the already killed to look in the eyes, to read the pictures of the killers etched on them, and that's when we got the idea to look out for Our Own Enemies, the men of the day before Clinch and me knew we got—why we thought we would see them anywhere near this place I am no longer sure—to see could we spy ourselves etched in them who we thrashed and we searched but never did find them, 1 Dead Boy looking much like another after the first dozen, and in fact we got turned around it was such a Thicket. I looked under a bush and there was not anything there but I could not stop looking under it, sir. I looked under it again, almost ready to crawl in there to get to the bottom roots wanting to see them so bad. I was in a terrible state of sottedness. Clinch pulled me on, and we was looking here and there and it seemed it must have taken hours but that can not be. Clinch pinched open the eyelids of the Dead Enemies, him all fascinated, and their jackets and boots was taken away and blouses, too, showing bony frames. In this 1, says Clinch, I see a bar-brawl and a medley of minor felonies, though no murder—but when I looked myself I saw only the flecks of that man's deep blue eyes around a Deep Black Spot. The 3rd Captain come then to ask what in *h-ll* was going on, what we were at, face pinching these carcasses, and the swing of that officer's sword was dipped in a fan of mirror mercury. I started to get ill watching it fan, and he asked Clinch most especially was the Company moving too quick, then, did its progress not meet his approval as he, Clinch, seemed to think he was in charge of that outfit, and Clinch said indeed he felt that if the rate of travel was okay with the others he would not speak against it. The 3rd Captain was not so keen on Clinch's straggles, so we went on through then with the rest, the 3rd Captain gone down the line, sword-swinging and mouth screaming, and Clinch called him a —Ordure

Eating Hell Spawn with a mind sharp as a Leading Edge of a Cannon Ball whose Bollocks should turn to Cubes and Fester at the Corners—and such in the manner he had, all after the 3rd Captain left, so I figured Clinch had taken back his common nature.[27]

We slid close behind another group on this strange day, and so kept on a long zag through this scorched wilderness till we crossed it, holding at a forest lip, and then overlooked a cleared farm—the first I had seen clear since the cars at the depot—and this open territory did sprawl and meander, sir. Gold light struck hilltops what showed dark foliages, and fields before was soft carpeted in bluegreen sward and I took all this in like a kind of a portrait with the sweating backs of a company of Georgians to the left, a nest of yellow flame on the upper right-hand, and every time or 2 a mounted officer or artillery gun [sprangling(?)] on a dust road what entered either side. The sight of a well-dug-in Enemy breastworks beyond the road though bedazzling to the eye was less than comforting on the other organs, and while I myself am not what you call a Overly Brave man, yet seeing all that fortification and the far clear spot in front of it, sir, I like to sh-t. I waited for Clinch to say something: words provoking and demeaning to our Foe yet cheering for the rest of us, such like that the faces of that Enemy was ugly enough to make a train take a dirt road, or that they, our Enemy, was more annoying than a Outhouse Fly, or at the least some statement as to their weakness, what would in general be 1 for cases such as this of the greased stick and dog's a— variety (as in their being too puny to pull the one out from the other) . . . almost anything but what he did say what was:

    —I have seen a goat roping, a rat killing, and a duck f-rt under water, but this beats anything I ever. Then light come on us free off the screen of trees and there was popping of guns and, between it, church bells from the hills—turns out it was a Sunday.

---

[27] Private Wallace employs again his "numbering system" for his commanders as noted, this one almost certainly James G. Shaw who replaced Lewis R. Moore killed at Little Round Top at Gettysburg.

That I have said and truly, sir, this about your son on this morning, plus also my telling about him resting on his arms at times and straggling, none of this should be taken as any sort of statement regarding your boy and his Great Bravery, for in truth such as he had was Profound and Strong, sir, and he knew No Fear in his life, at least until that Last day of it, the point being that though he Knew Fear he did not ever let it get in the way of his Duties, it was more a kind of sense of his own orneriness what did that. I am so tired, sir, I can not hardly stay upright, but it is January 29, sir, it was not out of being Afraid that Clinch had set himself against taking up arms and shooting (I will not say *murdering*) our Enemy. This matter of Jan 29 happened at Splinterville, this being our name for Winter Quarters, and, in fact, our name for most whatever shacks and tents we cobbled for shelter from the cold in freezing times. It is cold in this part of the country, sir, a unbelievable and unnatural kind of it, and Jan 29 in itself shows your own dead child's Bravery in Act and Willingness to undergo Privation for Comrades. We stood before that vast empty space, myself feeling odd and numb as I had very much the same felt at our Splinterville that winter, the light coming on us reminding me of the whipped up clouds of white at that place, and my breathing like it had been also at Splinterville, the air on that plain coming and stinging at my lungs like it held a white mist what moved in a rhythm, a blankness like a empty white, the shades of blue and streaks of blue and the morning sun low as had been the low evening sun of N. Virginia. And it was like Clinch forgot now how he took it when the officer mistreated him so rough, for he had loaded his rifle as he had not before, and I thought about his statement, of the goats, rats, and ducks, only the light of the valley was affecting me and making me shiver.

The smoke is in my eyes and I am yet clouded of mind, and I did not mean to scratch on with so long a tale, yet to know why Clinch refused to fight you must know about that cold. I shiver now to think of this yet, for the cold . . . it is to say that on a man's chilled meat of morning, the cold in these regions is enough for froze limbs (the

mere thought of it makes me *shake* hard), even your Clinch
seemed not untouched by this, for he called it a scut sort of
cold, a malignant Horn Beast of Freezing and Bitter, yet he
seemed more able to take it on than others owing to his well
upholstered frame. Still, he always spoke against it, saying
he would rather go in a battle any day than go in a winter
in Virginia, although on Jan 29 he changed his mind, but
these for reasons having to do with Honor and Deceit.

And back on the morning of that cold day he had been
speaking already against that cold as Pard left with his weapon
to go on a picket and Clinch was thinking about going too
to get out of the smoke of that shack we built, and also the
mess of the group what at that time was run by the man called
Peacock who died today just before your Clinch, Peacock
cooking at that time because Ward's nigger was dead, and this
Peacock's food was so much worse than that of the nigger,
it was considered more fatal than shot or shell. It might be
better to face a skirmish than a luncheon from Peacock, and
a bit of bacon after his boiling of it would cast no shadow, it
was like that.[28] But it was no quicker that Pard had left than
we heard a arousal, us standing around a small fire and feeling
after a breakfast of Peacock food not so much full as happy
to yet be alive, and it was from all over the 4th come word of
Attack, to gather haversacks and stores, and I got tingling, and
wanted to know should I run for Pard but they said he would
not be needed, what sounded odd, nor ammunition as all we
would desire was yet gathered around us in the [drenchy(?)]
ground, and I did not like the sound of this as the whole of
the terrain was covered in the most un-natural snow of a kind
they have in Virginia, it having come a wet dumper in the
night. I wanted nothing to do with this new summons, but the
buglers called parade then, the Colonel himself at the head of
it to address that parade. It was either Key or Carter—I never
much knew the difference between them—and we formed to

---

[28] My guess here, and it is only a guess, is that "Peacock" is Thomas
Bird, a member of the company listed as "killed at Chickamauga" in
Keith, *Hood's Texas Brigade*, 231. "Peacock's" demise is recorded by
Wallace on page 51 of this edition.

listen to this man's impassioned speech.[29] This colonel said
how he had all innocently that morning delivered paper to
the 1rst Texas—sheets of writing paper to lend a box of it to
the colonel over there who had expressed the strong need for
such writing material on the evening before—and our Colonel
did Harp in a Manner of Eloquence his belief that there never
had been *any* requirement for stationary by the 1rst but these
writing materials had but served as a Trick for enticing our
Colonel into their grips to receive a Sound Snowballing!

This news struck us as untoward—for a snowball cast

---

[29] Colflatt's reply to my second response to his second article on the
EW finds more to complain of here ("A 'Colonel' of Truth Unravels
the 'Wrapper': J. DeRossier's Snowballing Historical Fiasco." *Journal
of the Center for Southeast Texas Studies* 27 (Fall 1997), 387-94. Dr.
Colflatt finds it odd that Private Wallace does not distinguish between
these two figures since they come to us as very different in nature and
personality, each recording distinguished service with the 4th Texas,
each leading the regiment at different times. (At Splinterville, Carter
would have been second in command, under Key.) In fact, Colflatt's
answer to my previous answer notes how "someone who never served
his country would not understand the degree of identification between
troops and their regimental level officers" (Colflatt, "A 'Colonel' of
Truth," 389)—and refers to his own time in Kosovo under the much
beloved "Lt. Col Joe Anderson of the storied 82nd Airborne." I'm not
sure that failure to have participated in the Armed Forces *per se* makes
a person "someone who never served his country," but that aside, it is
true that these two officers appear to have been very different. John C.
G. Key, from the Goliad, Texas region, commanded the regiment from
July 1862 to April 1864, and while effective and brave, comes through
the record as rather colorless. Sergeant John Wunder, also of the 4th
Texas, records on the other hand that ". . . no officer in Hood's Texas
Brigade . . . achieved more universal affection and admiration . . ." than
Lt. Colonel Benjamin F. Carter. To me, given Private Wallace's poor
memory, his penchant for straggling, his general "distance" from high
ranking officers, as well as the circumstances of the EW's composition, this confusion between Carter and Key is not nearly enough
to cast doubt on the document as a whole. After Splinterville, both
officers were wounded at Gettysburg, Carter fatally. See Anne Scherer,
Editor, *Let Me Slide Back Home: A Memoir of John Earl Wunder in the
Fourth Texas Infantry,* (New York, Robinson, 1951).

against our colonel was, in fact, a snowball cast against All in the regiment—and he did yet show the effects of those flakes on the blades of his coat what he brushed at with the ledge of his glove—and it did raise Ire, most inflamed by our own Discomforts in this region of Awesome Cold as well, plus Peacock food, and no supplies . . . a thought that the offer of a thing of value from our own and respected officer (if it was Key he was a lot more respected than Carter[30]) should be met with such response caused all to rise in a Vow of Vengeance against a Act so Uncivil. So we did not stand long but went for haversacks and begin to fill these with snowballs, as most among the company had come from Other Climes before plunking in the county, and knew of such matters, plus the construction of the more deadly accurate ice-balls as well, them what Ward—himself born of a Tennessee family—later shook his head over, these being the sort what could harm a man, yet not so bad as the evil Clods some used that day. For myself and Clinch, we had neither the two of us made such missiles before, but found ourselves with the hang quick, and I'll say at this point in regards to the events of that Infamous day, there was at that time, I can promise, sir, none among the 4th who thought to place the addition of a Clod *inside* a snowball, not merely because of our Splendid Natures but also, coming from where we did, because of our being ignorant of the possibility even of trying out such treachery. Clinch and me heaved our haversacks onto our backs and went to join in.[31]

---

[30] Surely, Private Wallace has this backwards, Carter by all accounts being by far the more "backwoods and direct" of the two—and for that reason more generally thought of as having the troops' approval. Still, why would a forger place such evidence contradictory to the record in the EW, when it is admitted by the author that he does not recall which colonel it was?

[31] Dr. Hirschorn felt this portion of the narrative intimating that "Boys of the True South" would stoop to the unfair tactic of "ice clods" caused the EW's suppression in the 19th century. My personal belief is that critics then and now find another aspect of the EW more "offensive" than these clods (see below).

Our colonel somehow made a pact with the 5th who would join us in our assault so we set up a Screech and Holler, sir, and moved off, with your boy Clinch speaking as to the coldness of this enterprise, also taking part in it nonetheless as being better to Freeze in the Open than to suffocate in our smoked up shack, and the day was going to be a Fated one for him, sir, where his role would Loom Large, and I myself scuttled some behind the others, feeling as I did a little loose, I believe from drinking the water thereabouts. Ward's nigger had gone for heaven by then, killed I believe by that water, though set up in a warm house with a family Ward found him where he could take shelter out of elements, his nigger being a cultured one and somewhat unable to be treated to our style of life, plus worth a thousand dollars, yet lost always now for all the care Ward give him.

I can tell you, sir, only that the assault on the 1st was Swift and Sure, them surrendering promptly under a press of Great Numbers, and most of it happening before I got there, though I did see a mess of them making out for a copse of woods where we thought they might have gone to hide and set for a day of Ambush. I had stopped to relieve myself,[32]

---

[32] Colflatt posits this as an anachronism, noting that the phrase is never found in American documents before the twentieth century. Alan Colflatt, "This Time It's Personal: Jules DeRossier and the 'Equinox Wrapper'," *Journal of the Center for Southeast Texas Studies* 26 (Fall 1996), 376. Just how he was able to check every urination reference before the twentieth century he does not mention, but I basically agree with him. It makes most sense here to assume Wallace is simply writing about resting: i.e., "relieving himself." DeRossier, "You're Welcome to Your Own Opinion . . . ," 45. It is admirable that Colflatt does not take the tack of less sophisticated critics who feel it impossible that any Southern "gentlemanly soldier" could be so foul-mouthed as Michael "Clinch" Williamson. Although many Confederate records were lost in a Richmond fire after the war, Union army documentation in the National Archives demonstrates widespread courts martial for language much like that Wallace's comrade evinces in the EW, and it is hard to imagine that the expletive vocabulary would have been much different between the two armies. Speaking of language which might seem anachronistic, but in fact is not, I was

yet the events from that point began to slip free, as some among the guard in seeing the snow-tracks of them what had lighted out pointed to how them prints showed bare feet in this freezing cold, and all present had a immediate and clear opinion spring to lips: —*Arkansans!*—and all made also the quick surmise that these pickets had gone to warn the Porkers of the 3rd Regiment for either retaliation against us or a retreat before we could assault them, so a assault got planned against that group even where none had been planned before. For such was the plain effect of that day, sir, created in my eye solely through a sort of madness of what I can but call a Snowballing Fever what I had likewise caught even before ever letting fly one ball against Foe. In a moment all got the same message, and the regrouped and re-joined regiments of Texas, having now forgot the icy pounding and even the insult of the stationary, was bound together in common, the 1st, 4th and 5th gone to seek Arkansans where they lived and hid.[33]

Snow cracked under feet and we lugged up a froze creek till through branches there stood the familiar sleepy tents and ramshackle sheds of Third regiment, a smoke puff sometimes rising from a rough chimney thrown up out

---

somewhat shocked to discover the most common phrase of offense among those archived courts martial to be "Suck my dick." See Edward A. Walker Jr. *The Unexpurgated Civil War: Sex, Law, and Society in the War Between the States* (Berkeley, Wald Press, 1990).

[33] Where did the Battle of Splinterville take place? Sergeant John Wunder records picket duty during this time "at the Old Buchanan Home two miles below the City of Fredericksburg, on the south bank of the river." That would have been "Winchester," one of Fredericksburg's most elegant antebellum homes, owned by attorney Arthur Buchanan, the center of a sprawling 2100 acre estate. *Let Me Slide Back Home*, 181. This aligns fairly well with drummer Samuel A Wickham's recollection that Co. F, 5th Texas "wintered on a high ground near the Rappahannock River, just below Fredericksburg." *A Rebel Boy Tells All*, (Austin, Deep Eddy, 1974), 45. I place the battlefield a bit south of the present day Sylvania Heights subdivision. "Winchester" burned after the war, and an Elks Lodge is built on its site.

of irregular stones, these Arkansans being, it was claimed, distrustful our Forces might really stay in one part a whole winter and so ready to pull out any moment but now feeling sorry they did not have better shacks. Wild fields surrounded their huddling coops and lean-tos in a hollow bowl of ground what must have been for them the best they could find to remind them of their carved out Home Territories, and a Reign of Peace Hovered over this Little Settlement, yet it was but a Mocking Phantasm, for at a signal the men of Texas crested the rim of the bowl and poured down on those Porkers, many of whom it turned out were yet asleep and covered up with every scrap they had to get under, and when the racket drug them out of their nests in the light of morning these figures in their poor wraps did meet with the most Awful Sacrifice to flying snow ball and ice and floating powdery snow. After less than scant minutes they had been erased to Spectral Outline, many surrounded before they could patty-cake fashion even the first ball together to retaliate and then they throwed up their frosted limbs to cover faces. A song did *rise* sir, I heard it there coming from us plus also the conquered's *Wail*, it was a breath of Defeat blowing out of them, goggled down on knees as before a Avenger of Man. It has give me a vision I yet hold, a scene of Struggle, sir, and Bitter Pain, with dark suspense of Reason, and grim and terrible Panorama. And not over by a moment neither as the force of it by this hour was yet unstoppable in a way we could not understand but had merely to be borne along with, the fire of it did gleam in your now dead and gleamless dead boy's eyes all exaggerated by the glasses. —I'll have a officer, said he to me, —And pelt him, but I was watching him close, making sure he did not "clinch" anything from these poor hill people—though, in truth, sir, there was nothing to be removed from them and I could besides not see a officer among them though this came possibly through them all being so ghostly piled and whitened with the flecks of snow.

Next come the vicious forenoon assaults—them Arkansans, poor and frigid but game, going with us then against the Georgia Brigade of Anderson's, and a howling did go up with murderous Rage of Tone, sir, also fierce expression . . . such that those Georgians for certain would not be caught unawares but knew we was coming and made ready, there was no way they could not nor the country thereabouts as well know our plans, the air filled with Shrieks as we wheeled a line against their position along a dip of land—well chose by them it turned out as offering no cover to our Assault, and the air was filled as well with snowballs, ice balls, ice slivers, the snow come and burst around me in a blank glaze what your boy called Mad and Stunning. I lost all fear for myself dodging the force of it, flying down off that well defended rise, and I wondered yet was I even myself in those moments, or someone else watching Henry Wallace from afar. Our assault come on, me lowering my head down my collar to fend off the worst, with sound like Pattering Roar, or rain after thunder passed, yet times too of silence what made no sense in them circumstances, and we Screamed, I believe, half to fill that silence for it was colder than the wind and ice itself. There come a long roll like from many drums at a time, and the sound of it swept and swelled out through ground and trees, yet I had no fear, could see little, but heard Ward say *Hark!* what was something he would say from time to time, *D'ye hear it?* he said. *It is clods!* And we did not know, Clinch nor myself, of what he spoke, till one cut out across my wrist, and I could tell it, then, they were throwing hard rocks at us—frozen mud at the least, the 2nd Captain being set down on his trousers with one of these dark missiles in his hand, plus a worm of bright blood on his forehead, and he lifted and peered at this clod as a man holds a false coin.

—*Why those can put your eye out*, said Ward and we come up then to their battlements, feeling Certainty of Indignation greater than that we'd possessed since first leaving Camp Van Dorn, our having been give now the Duties of Men to rush ahead or Face Annihilation, Harm, even Blindness from this Scourge.

Running at them, these clods mixed with snow from the treacherous Peanut Eaters pattered hard, sent splints of mud what white-frosted my shoes and ankles, and it was

not till later I learned from them while examining this day
in our hours of more calm that they had as a method taken
to aiming a bit *short* of where they thought we was, having
a Idea we Texans would *run into* such barrage and seal our
Doom—what Clinch pointed out as proof we had again
been misunderestimated, this time on how slow we could
run. The 2nd Captain made it to a space below their fortress,
pulling up those of us nearby, saying then words what thrill
me now yet to think of, him being no longer around to
echo them, —*Let us see what is in this thing, boys,* said he,
and stood with sword drawn when he did, cutting at snow
and mud, one leg crooked up their wall, so over we went,
facing the worst of their barrage head-in (except for Clinch),
a wall of it, sir, or blizzard as I would later feel south of
Suffolk but nothing of its kind nor coldness in my life had
ever touched me up to that part and these balls but *froze*,
sir, it was a terror of Ice and chilling Hellsnow, all become
a smear though your dear dead Clinch was one who stood
it well. Clinch went a— first into this onslaught—for what
part of man provides better to withstand such pounding,
and Clinch's more able than most?—him backing in harm's
way hanging his fire to improve chances of surviving that
burst and give them back their own when he cleared the
top, for we had by design held some reserve snowballs yet
until that moment of Offensive, and we let the Georgians
have it, sir. Though it was in a fit of Exhaustion after such a
tramp through the Deep White I got there and snowballed
hard, and we sprung on our Enemy just as he had shot his
last, the goober-pickers even then [scrabbling(?)] to roll more
balls, nary a one admitting later to have taken any sort of
mud or frozen soil from that obvious gash in the ground
there among them, and it was Arkansas all over, for some of
them we would gang up, ten Texans and Arkansans to one
peanut eater, and we pasted him.

It is a wonder there is any intoxicant including
yesterday morning's poisonous variety what has so scrambled
my thoughts having any Power greater than that found
in Victorious Action, sir, we fair danced, then, on the
battlements, we sung out for the 2nd Captain's benefit *Let's*

see what's Inside! What's in this Thing, Boys? and the like, with some of the company propping foot on prostrate Georgian or two. My knees are weary and stiff, and I did not mean to go on so, this message must look to you to be of a odd length, yet I must speak of Clinch, I believe I heard him repeat it, them words, at intervals on that day (but not yesterday, his day of finality[34]). I can imagine Clinch saying it yet in the Vaulted Halls of the Paradise to where he is now retired: *Let's see what's Inside this Thing* and shoving in, a— first, and the Second Captain [waiting on] him there. For a time we forgot all including cold for the run and exertions had brought us to a point of steaming garments, we forgot our fatigue, the cuts from fatal clods, the pasty howls of a occasional peanut farmer yet arised in alarm. Here we come to gather together in a mass and sink to rest, lean on sacks and breath out smoke. Mack leaned his head back, and Clinch and Donovan and Ward and myself, all of us coated over and white, and I saw that Mack's bottom lip—clipped by some clod—had purpled over and so quivered. Some grumbled of a poor Texan's Disadvantage at these Winter Exertions—for who would consider to pack a stone inside of snow?—and Mack,

---

[34] Here Colflatt adds "internal inconsistency" to his list of offenses "proving" the EW a forgery. The EW is dated September 20, the same day as the battle, and so Michael Williamson's death would not have been "yesterday" but rather "this morning." Putting aside the foolishness of placing so much weight on such a subtle discrepancy, I have personally taken a sheet of wrapping paper, cut to a two-foot width, and copied out . . . *not the entire manuscript*—but a representative sample of the EW's contents. *Under optimum conditions* (using the table, not the floor, of my own well-lit kitchen, a No 2 Ticonderoga Pencil, an electric sharpener . . . a diet drink by my side), I estimate it would take me at a good eight hours to replicate the entire forty-foot-long letter, and must suppose that it took Private Wallace at least that long for the original composition. It is nearly certain that this portion was written, then, after midnight, on into the morning of the 21st. Is it beyond reason to assume Wallace would recognize this via the merest consultation with "Pard?" (See the silver watch pages 9, 28.) He likewise mentions the sunrise on the 21st, page 62. The EW contains no internal inconsistency in regards to this matter.

his bottom lip shook in anger and Peacock filled his pipe, yet soon we were on the move again, and *Hark!* said Ward and *Hark!* we all said, for there was movement now. *Hark! Hark!* There was to be more *action*, sir, this bringing with it Life to send off Woe. We must yet storm them hills. Them Georgians, you see, had now been absorbed, their officers all spilled out of their hutches and sheds, the 2nd Captain sent a man for our colors, we'd do this right, tested as we were in the mere skirmishes of morning.[35] It became clear we'd be going north what we come to know as the drums started and the bugles did and we lined up on our colors and how we did set our mark towards that encampment, the white outposts could be seen only barely through some oaks—it was to be McLaw's Division against Hood's.

We must storm the hills. We must and we rose to parade a line on our flags, a few breathless moments seemed a long pocket in the time what followed, it took us a while to organize while the cold yet creeped, and finally we moved in a surge, a mansion hove by us, pretty and Virginian, on rising ground, yet the land in front mashed down and give a tramping by our having bivouacked here the winter, so we mashed it more going to give the Nth Carolinians what we felt their due, though looking back now I can not see they ever really done anything to us, it was all started with the 1rst and that stationary.[36] Yet the hedge and the shrubs of

---

[35] The EW, perhaps more than any other extant document, demonstrates in detail the way the Battle of Splinterville escalated (snow-balled?) over the course of January 29. Wickham supports Wallace, but begins with smaller units, describing this "greatest snowball fight of the ages" as spreading from "company to company, to regiment from regiment, to brigade from brigade, to divisions by battling forces absorbing one another as they passed from place to place . . . until the whole of Longstreet's Corps was snow-battling." *A Rebel Boy Tells All*, 52.

[36] Maj. Gen. Lafayette McLaws' Division was made up principally of *South* Carolinians, but Pvt. Wallace labels them as *Nth Carolinians* throughout—again demonstrating admirable internal consistency. Private Wallace also, in his misuse of the apostrophe, consistently misspells McLaws' name.

that planter did go down no matter and I saw in all the steam of our passing a face at window, the face of a old man yet holding on it a look what a boy might show when caught at something for what he knew he would later catch h-ll, and that not making much sense under the circumstances.[37]

While our line did go, it was not such certain assault at first, with a hour or more marching and countermarching before those officers had us *arranged*, more troops and reinforcements come from all directions, pouring in to support the Nth Carolinian Foe, too, all more or less dusted with snow depending on the amount of action they had seen so far. Them what appeared all clean and bare got our derisive jeer as cowards and green, and the Arkansans was the most vicious in stating this, being now the most earnest in seeking Violence of Snow against Man.

Our orders come at last and we moved double quick past a wood and into a larger field what sloped gentle to a dry gully then rose the same way the further side.[38] Over the acres, in full view, it was all of them, McLaw's Division, some maybe hiding to the left in some trees skirting that point. The 2nd Captain shouted out to us over the drums to hold back, time our volleys so there would be snow ever in the air, we would make it a mite hot for them with snow, and as we come in close it was clear them Carolinians had the idea of getting the officers and flag-bearers first, because it was that corporal and the Second Captain what got bursting balls [windering(?)] them in a cloud and a awesome pounding under it. I held back some to pack more snow and shook my numb fingers and caught up a breath of the fine mist from those burst snowballs what stung at my lungs in a

---

[37] That this should be Arthur Buchanan's "Winchester" is not likely, the structure being deserted by this time and basically ransacked. See *Let Me Slide Back Home, A Memoir of John Earl Wunder,* 182.

[38] Although unable to prove it, I strongly suspect that this area is now the concrete culvert noted on modern maps as "Emerson Slough." It serves as drainage for a number of housing subdivisions in this part of suburban Fredericksburg, including Sylvania Heights. Exactly where along the slough would be conjecture added to conjecture.

way what made me think myself most powerful and moved by the rhythm of this Spectacle. —How grand this is, said I to Clinch, and he said it was a Blessing to be there to see it and hear it, too (for the band had come out by then, sir, and was playing). Clinch said it was good snow was so cold else men should get too fond of heaving it at each other, and I saw all: each shade of that crystal snow, the blueness of streaks inside it, a slant of light as low afternoon sun come through trees, the brown ranks of our ongoing file. We come up close to Their own line in a frenzy but could see soon trouble on the right, amongst those our Georgian and Arkansan troops positioned there, it was some *other* trees, sir, some we hadn't really figured into as a problem, but it was from here McLaw's outriders started to pour, *Cavalry!*—and Mack in a panic said we was outflanked, now, would be enfiladed, but Clinch told him them hillbillies would hold for they had better, else soon all would be lost and there would be suffering. The Georgians, the Arkansans, they should have made a run for it and fell back under the onslaught of the horses and snowballs, sir, but instead those dear boys wheeled in the fading light—it was such a thing—they turned their line without a slack in their own snowball heaving, turned against them snorting horses and the riders who could not, after all, carry too many snowballs at a time, all the while the Arkansans and Georgians closing up gaps caused by them who had give out under the terror of assault, men dropping, dropping, holding up their hands, but it was brave and they saved us for the cavalry went back in the trees when they'd been near ready to roll us up like a rug.[39] Then it seemed each various instrument of snow and wrath got unleashed at once, everything and everyone taking part, from the left, right, behind. In a open space our men lurched savage and launched their snowballs into white nothing what covered all, never seeing who was there only heaving for glory.

---

[39] Ramsey estimates that by this point in the day 12,000 veterans of the Army of Northern Virginia were taking part in a "free-for-all snowball battle royal." *From Here to Appomattox*, 110-11. McLaws' Division must have been taking its snowballing seriously to bring out mounted troops in these conditions.

We could have held out but a little while at our own place, the bottom of this gully-crossed field, but our fire must have told for when the Nth Carolinians charged with bugle, drum and ice we opened on them yet and forced them to the right in a swerve, yet they kept coming. Every time I raised up my arm to throw I got covered in a onslaught, but I just thought *there goes me* and let fly. On the left, we could see it about to go, a Captain was there imploring and threatening and sometimes begging but his men scootching back the whole time. He pulled out his pistol on them at the last but it was no use so he flung himself on the snow and kicked a fury. Our Own fine Captain held us to our business here this day and with his sword snipped at the twig ends of grasses poked through the tramped snow and he paced and dodged and was pleased.

They come in fierce in a charge what swept all before, then at the last come some fresh stragglers, they'd heard the ruckus[40] they come to beef up our ranks, and we knew then it was press on or meet doom so with these added numbers to cheer us we begin our surge what was when the 2nd Captain said how *If this line falls then we was goners*, for we had reached the *Point of Cold Consequences* and it was *Time to be Took Up with Recklessness* which all thought was just [fine words(?)] then it was your Clinch hisself who pointed out with his fingers the spot where we stood and said it was *The Last Ditch in this Place* and so that made it the time for *Our Last Ditch Effort* and when the company heard all these statements, it could not be held back.

We dealt out the cold to them our aggressors as the sun dropped, thousands of snowballs got hurled and when they burst a dense layer formed what dropped but more of this frigid mix on all, and coming out of it we could see men as if in mist, we could count every star on their battle flags, though all was cased in white, and them Nth Carolinians had

---

[40] A Union cavalry regiment on picket duty on the Federal side of the Rappahannock heard the commotion as well, and, fearing an attack of some kind, saddled their mounts and prepared to defend their position. See Keith, *Hood's Texas Brigade*, 84.

pulled their hat brims down to shade their eyes from sun and snow, and we saw their very faces under those brims. I singled out one after another while I worked hard at it and admired certain long brown icicles what hung from mouths and beards. Rise and fire said somebody but it was not needed, for like phantasms we stood, our snowballs shrieked, the band played "Bonnie Blue Flag," the field before us changed as by some Unnatural Act of Mystery for in those moments what had been occupied before with charging host was of a sudden clear, erased white, the ground strode with prostrate forms of men, sometimes a arm raised up in supplication. The Nth Carolinians got blotted from the scene, sir, and we could make out the distant backs of them what run, though hard to see as our own breaths come in a vapor to obscure. From the mist come a man waving hands in token of surrender, and this was a officer, I think it might have been a Regiment Colonel who had been fool enough to lead that point blank charge, but we never found out for sure because of Clinch as Clinch was on him in a heat, demanding his sword what this Lofty Official was loathe to give over to a mere private and this got Clinch in high snit as sun went down, such that we had to cart him off or all be put away in irons, that is how mad he was, and it is rather a strange fact then, sir, that we broke away in the dark to some woods and sat around under the moon and cried. This I mean to say in its real sense, we wept and moaned with tear and grimace of sorrow, and I am not sure from where it come or who it started with but it was Mack and Peacock and West and Donovan and your now dead boy Clinch and myself, we sat snow-covered like ghosts, we shivered like fish, we had a big boo hoo.[41]

---

[41] While willing for the most part to assign a motive of genuine scholarly skepticism to Colflatt and Dickinson for their obsession with attacking the legitimacy of the letter, it is difficult not to believe they also act at least in part from the kind of misplaced patriotism evinced by those who have found this passage and a similar mention of this incident on page 62 the most objectionable portions of the EW. The gentlemanly Hirschorn's "snow-clod theory" aside, this—the image of soldiers of Hood's Texas Brigade sitting and weeping—created the true

I do not know how long this went, sir, but we did break ourselves out of it, and I am recalled that I was scribbling more of yesterday's doings before going off into those of January 29, because it was from that very day that the sword was snatched from his grip that Clinch took it to himself to think there was no point in him serving these masters more than they had to be, that he was no longer trustful of them, sir, that they were besides people of a type what put themselves above others, all the kind of thinking what at that time did not make much sense to me, for who can even spend a minute with someone with the gifts from nature of Major General John Bell Hood—who I mention as example—and not feel he is in the presence of a *someone* and a someone *out of the ordinary*, a Man above others if not in all ways then in many and demanding of respect on

---

storm of controversy for him when he first encountered the holograph and paraphrased some of its contents in print, and this "critical analysis" has continued to the present day. It is, in fact, this incident at the Battle of Splinterville which has caused many to label the EW a forgery even before examining it. Many in the 1990's constructed elaborate rationales for the alleged hoax, and although few match his shrillness of tone, most argue along the lines of a Mr. Albert Wicke writing in *Southern Breezes Magazine* (Spring 1993, 12). Mr. Wicke quotes General Patrick Ronayne Cleburne, one of Hood's officers who died at the unnecessary slaughter which was the battle of Franklin, Tennessee, (an afternoon and evening in November, 1864 during which six thousand Confederate troops died in six fruitless charges). I quote: "Cleburne accurately predicted the present state of Southern demise when he warned that loss of the Revolt would mean the 'loss of all we now hold most sacred . . . . Our youth will be taught by Northern school teachers, and will learn from Northern school books their version of the War.' How accurately this general predicted a time when we can watch on TV Southern fathers who comfort their children at the airport as they send their Southern mothers off to fight and die in Iraq [Desert Storm]. Surely there is no icon for this a*ssault on manhood* and final outcome of *cultural annihilation* more representative than the ludicrous scene set forth in this alleged and contemptuous letter." (italics in original.)

field of battle. Clinch took it bad, and did not load nor raise his rifle against a Enemy after but continued to march with us, I think because he felt it was a protection to myself, and for this I will be grateful ever, for he did not kill but was always at my side since that day what we come to call the Battle of Splinterville.

But sir, yesterday, our second in this field, we stood before that awesome *blank space* before our Enemy, we made ready our attack—there was to be no snowballing here—and I myself would have like to stood and pondered a while on your boy's Unnatural State of Panic—still thinking, as I was, on his statement of the goats, rats and ducks, only the light of the valley was affecting me, as had the light from the forest before when we had been looking at the dead Enemies spread out in every place. This light, then, sir, so like that of Nth Virginia, I know it fell from the sun and was of a type common to every day experience—it being the same sun shown down then what had since Bible days—it, this light, appeared as awakened for its day of work much as your soon to be totally dead boy Clinch and myself had been woke up—*way too early*, and I was surprised at finding it—that light—also like us in being full of hopes and plans but these about to go pap, and it did not till that moment pass to me how light itself could be so full of worry and sensitive feeling. I stood dazzled and attempted to form a manner of cheering response for them poor rays—Clinch seeming in no mood to do so—but then we got prodded and all walked out and in the clear, myself starting to have a real scare going then—for me, though, unlike your boy, a more common state when entering such situations—realizing how the brandy was coming near rendering *incapacitation*, especially if Clinch was approaching a state of dismay and him and me had got to the point of searching corpse eyes and comforting sunbeams . . . you can tell of my befuddlement, sir, yet it is the clear case that at that moment I knew there would be no winter fun but true trouble here, and yet I had not took it serious, but imbibed in the brandy—and oh, how I wished it possible, then, to dis-imbibe it, what a mistake that yet causes my head to pound and brings on weakness. I scratch ahead to tell you of what I set out to, yet must point out how of a sudden it Terrorized me that for the sake of a pick-me-up I had plunked myself in a Dangerous Position in a Open Part with Lead Pouring In and nothing to hide behind save grass and that grass Very Short. If it was not for the handful of bark tripes what give my stomach a rind of protection there is no telling what might have followed from that brandy, so this is 1 more way I say it was your boy saved my life this day and while it was also him endangered me, in the end it does not matter.

Our squad come quick on in a area in which minie balls buzzed, and—This is just what I need, said Clinch, him being drunk and woozing as myself, the both of us in a state. Shells come flying, then, from off right and left, lead screaming, and we reached the road in moments' time, sheeted there in a cloud of parched dust what hid all.[42] To my side I heard Pard's Demented Boot, the sole of it near off, ker-flick, ker-flicking, and I heard my own gaggling of throat from trying to breath, but as to other sights or tones I was uncertain. It took a long time to cross that scorchy road-bed swirled in dust. At one point Mack says I hope this is not where I meet the bullet what has my name writ on it and I waited for Clinch's response what I knew near now by heart as it was automatic—words to the effect that as Mack was hisself a illiterate no such bullet could ever harm him—only all your Clinch said was *silence*. I was worried about him, sir. It happened to Peacock here, the dust come off his jacket in a spray where the ball twigged him, he fell to ground but we pressed on.

When we got clear of dust the company was scrambled, nobody where they was before, our little group kiltering off

---

[42] The La Fayette/Chattanooga Road, called today "Lafayette Road." Because of the "Terrible Gap" in the Union Forces which Private Wallace encounters below, we have a far better chance of locating him on the second day of battle. From the Chickamauga and Chattanooga National Military Park Headquarters, head south on Lafayette Rd. to Dyer Rd, turn right, and drive about 100 yards. This is the approximate position of the "well-dug-in Enemy breastworks" which Company L faced on the morning of September 20.

different ways, and it was not like the same world as distant trees was dressed now in corduroy suits and we walked under a sky blue as a parlor shade. I watched the log fortification before me come closer, halving its distance from me, halving its distance again with a regularness like that of a stick broke over knee took up and broke over knee again, strange and quiet direct to the front though guns cracked at the far right, such that I knew They was in there, They was waiting and going to look us [in the] face before our slaughter, and I was thinking all these things, sir, and knowing their direct inevitability, yet did not flounder though I admit I had at other times in the past floundered in various ways or at least held back, or at the very least shrunk my own head down into my own collar like that would help. None of this occurred to me to do on this day, sir, I walked on so near cutting the distance between me and the Enemy's trench I could not cut it more without crossing over in it, and I wanted to *see* them fellows, then, to get with them and fight —so I did, I did cross over into them logs and where they'd dug up the earth in a little rise, and the surprise was when I looked in there, and when I climbed that trash, there was no one there, there was no one standing in nor holding that place at all. It was Empty, sir, the Enemy being *not at all there* such that I had to blink to understand, and the emptiness at that fortification was 1, then, I finally pushed my face in happy with satisfaction, as a man is when he can sleep late for there is nothing much pressing that day, everything was going to go right. I verily sniffed in the fact of our Enemy's *Not Being* and asked Clinch what did he make of it, however he was not close to me at all but lying only a short ways beyond the road—your dead boy Clinch had got shot through the brains and fact was I missed even seeing it.[43]

---

[43] Here the EW provides an on-the-scene chronicle of one of the greatest strategic errors of the American Civil War—an important eyewitness record overlooked by those raising controversy over its account of the Battle of Splinterville. Responding to an ambiguous order from Union Commanding General William Starke Rosecrans at 10:45 A.M. on September 20, Brigadier General Thomas J. Wood

It was us and some from among the Georgians who overleaped this barricade, and the most went halloing and chasing up a incline after more trouble, but as for me, Clinchless of a sudden, I crawled at the top of the piled posts and dirt and then went in a dug ditch—the eerie quiet of your dead boy communicating to me a message I could not understand as it was one I was unaccustomed to hearing from him—and so I could not enjoy this our breakthrough. The strong burning of my ear-tips plus that of tongue and lungs, all brandy-caused, now had a escort of snapping in my bowels, and this caused me to lean to make a stream of foul and liquid brackish brandy-smelling oyster juice direct on the spadework of our Enemy, I un-imbibed after all, yet was afflicted.

While the work of this morning has took but little space to describe it took less to occur—though this cannot be as the sun soon burnt in near center of sky, as near the center as it could (it being that low-sunned, right-on-balance season of light to dark of the Autumn Equinox), and the day was warmed, had turned to summer temperatures, with feather clouds going over and slick blood in that trough below, a scene of a lovely day on one hand with the bloodied pile of my friend and your boy Clinch on the other—it was all as some kind of dance hall joke.

I could tell him from amongst the other handful of

---

pulled three brigades of troops out of line to fill a gap to his left, even though he knew no such gap existed. This action created a real break nearly a half mile wide through which eight Southern Brigades, including the Texas Brigade, almost immediately poured. In his defense, Wood had been criticized earlier in the day by Rosecrans for not complying promptly enough to orders. Ultimate blame for the disaster which followed has been hotly debated, and the "horrible gap" appears prominently in memoirs of Rosecrans, Wood, and even Rosecrans' chief of staff at Chickamauga, James A. Garfield, later twentieth president of the United States. See Wendell Kusmer, *The Middle Years of the War*; S. M. Oshinsky, *Chain of Command: Civil War Generals and Their Staffs*; Anthony Ortizar, ed. *The Citadel Atlas of American Wars*, Maps 14(d), (e). Clearly, Private Michael "Clinch" Williamson could not have picked a more unlikely time or place to be struck down by what must have been a stray round.

dead out there—his spectacles was what made me sure that was him, he had got drilled through the skull with the specs disturbed not one bit—and as his head gore bubbled into soil I wondered at the complete unutility of glasses on a corpse, and I stood waving your Clinch goodbye, till Mack told me —Get down fool you can yet be killed, though, sir, fact was our Enemy had fled out of there very fast.[44] Mack was breathing hard beside me, and said, —Henry you are looking queer, and we cannot help Clinch now, and you are seeming worn and pale, besides, and should rest, and I said—looking out at your boy's gummy mound (it was blood all to h-ll out there around his head, sir—or, as Clinch once said of a like scene in Nth Virginia: Slicker than two eels f—king in a tub of sh-t, what I knew he would never say again)—looking out there I said to Mack: —I do not see how Clinch could do what he's doing better with our help than he is without, and Mack said, —You perhaps should go to have a lie down.

For me I was too drunk to have a fall down—forget lie down—but Mack left though promised to return, then he went with the others to chase at the Enemy up the hill, and this, sir, was the point in which my day began to take on complexions of the bizarre.

For I did not stay and wait for Mack at that empty barricade nor make a march for the hill he was going at either but begun instead to walk a complete other direction, to brood and feel unsoldierly, thinking I had done enough for one day. In fact I was pondering how the Kernel of this whole Scene, was I to peel its shell, might have no Seed at all

---

[44] When Confederates poured through the "open door," forces under Brigadier George P. Buell and Colonel Sidney Barnes had little recourse but to flee. These included soldiers of the Eighth Kansas, Fifteenth Wisconsin, and Twenty-Fifth Illinois. Union troops made two other significant stands on into the long afternoon of the 20th, but most scholars feel this massive breakthrough made the result at Chickamauga a foregone conclusion. See Frank Goldfield, *Chickamauga: A Day-Trip Guide*, (Athens, Pines Press, 1990) 130; Neil Walton, *A Warrior Poet: The Life of William H. Lytle*, (New York, Discovery Press, 1996) 372.

to its center. The grass went under me and I over it, moving away from the company and brigade as they had gone and shaked out to engage a hill bristled with trees and guns.[45] I felt a breeze off the afternoon dry the sweat on my hair, and I was at once tired, yet [more settled] of stomach, yet also dissatisfied. The world was taking its own breaths as I stepped on it and I had to watch or else tip over from its puffing so, as it would take only a tiny flick of that valley to topple me—throw me and the dance-stepping corpses and the exclamation points what was stalks of trees and the lively grasses and the lively artillery batteries, haybarns, tobacco shacks, mules, red-painted farmhomes and breastworks made of sticks and logs . . .

. . . all of this would go a tumble should the ground decide to take in a real big breath, skulls would get cracked, sir, spines snipped, shingles blown off roofs and like that. This was also when I met up with Hood, that meeting what solidly made me believe I should set down the occurrences of this battle, to get straight, especially to you, about the death of Clinch your boy, and Mr. Williamson, I can say I expected to meet Jeff Davis before I did Hood. I thought the Major-General still in hospital in Richmond, healing from that shell what had near punched off his arm in Sth Pennsylvania. Yet I wandered before coming upon him, him on his fine horse, and by this time the rippling pages of hillsides was making comments, mostly telling them only to themselves they being the only ones twittering over them, and the clouds likewise had songs going—rambling pieces what twisted one inside another, all unrelated tunes and vapor-like, while the wind give a cooling recital from the West. I chuckled. The death of your killed boy, the shock it give me in my state of Near Stupor caused this my freakish reflection on the nature of the Living World, and I entered such a flip-handed condition I come to believe I had only just then been woke up, sir—that I had spent my times up to that point, starting back with growing up on the Lower

---

[45] Almost certainly the heavily-wooded "Snodgrass Hill" area, still clearly visible to battlefield visitors.

Coushatta and the fights I used to get into there, on up to Dumphries, Gaines' Mill, Malvern Hill, Rocky Top, that long train ride to here from Virginia . . . to my being face down in wet leaves that very morning . . . *all* of that had been a dream of emptiness from what I was now just awoke.[46]

The horizon had to get into it, too, pushing through the trees to tell its little horizontal episodes . . . for everything was talking now, sir, and it was not much the substance what tickled me of what the horizon said—for it was not at all anything to speak of—but more the manner of delivery what doubled me over in a hollering fit, how features got pushed up from the frank flat of the whole, and all these stories and songs I heard was of that fashion. I could not find anyone to share this with as it seemed everyone was a stranger and moving fast, and it did not matter as about all I would have to say to anyone about these jokes and songs would be something like: —*Never mind you would have to be here to appreciate it.*

Waves of what I (at that particular passing) took to be troublesome men run up the hill to meet head-on the yellow fire and smoke of the other troublemakers to the top of it,[47] and I had to think Pard and Mack and Ward swarmed in that number though it was impossible to say, and a horse pulling a caisson near run me level but I figured *Oh well* and I just turned from it, not wanting even to see such comedy,

---

[46] Almost certainly Wallace means "Little Round Top" at Gettysburg where the 4th Texas was heavily engaged. Detractors resist labeling this an anachronistic reference to the Osborne Brothers classic "Rocky Top" (now official song of the State of Tennessee), but Colflatt loses all restraint regarding another passage, see footnote, page 58.

[47] Confederate forces met strong resistance at Snodgrass Hill. The actual chronology of the battle is difficult to follow in the EW, as events unfolded much faster than Private Wallace here presents them. Most certainly, Company L was one among those troops of the 4th who got too far ahead of the rest of Longstreet's Corps and experienced enfilading fire from Union troops, this after being told personally by Hood to "Go" and "Keep ahead of everything," his usual approach to any military situation. O.R.A. Series I, Vol. 30, Part II, p.511-15.

for it looked to me to be the very thing what your boy, little Clinch, had called it just a bit earlier in the day, what was in fact *murder*. *Foolish Murder*, sir, without reason or cause, these men disturbing the inhaling world below them for no gain, me just now picking up on it, though I had been at it a while myself at various places, and . . . .

. . . and the only reason it had not come to me before was maybe it was just too obvious—I had been in those cases kind of caught like a ant in a web only what I was truly caught up in was acts of murder, sir! I was excited during them times—not thinking right, nor taking out the time for walking or thinking and quite possibly asleep myself as well—*Sleep Murdering*, sir—taken into the dream of it without realizing. And I *saw* the cow, sir, and by that I mean I was took up in a state of drunkeness so fierce I *saw* it, the cow, as if before me though it had been a year since it happened, the one me and Quick come up on in a field,[48] splayed so with its cow eyes watching the sky but the rest just a exploded skin, sir, not knowing what hit it it got hit so hard so fast, not having a way to understand such a piece of metal flying, living and chewing blades a moment, drilled through the next, the juices of it spread in a cone shape all in one direction, and sure it was my thinking on that cow caused me then to have thoughts on something else I cannot describe what lasted many instants, that cow's skin peeled from its leg so it looked a woman's skin beneath, the belly blown, wet packages what was its life all spilled. I can not describe it but perhaps best only say it come to me how I did not then doubt but definitely Clinch should have included the horses and cows in his list, should have counted up both sides of the dead in a total, included pigs, tramped shrubbery, broke twigs, anything else come to its demise in this dream story—all of that should have been in on one count, just as all when covered with the whiteness of snow looks much

---

[48] Readers might remember this cow (page 13), but I can find no other references to "Quick" in the EW or the official records of Company L. If a nickname, it seems the sort which might be based on a personal trait rather than a surname.

the same, it is hard to tell a difference between one man and another in all that whiteness, you have to play it by trust to find a man to fight in snow.[49] And it reminds me how your boy had such a fury on, sir, and a anger when that white covered colonel refused him the sword. Your Clinch flexing his fingers in one hand and holding in the other a mallet sized snowball what he raised over his head, and making his demands, and I thought on Clinch and Splinterville as I began to wander yet feel weak, like *I had been hit*, like I had lost blood, yet could find no place on me—as I looked—where there was a wound. And the thing was, as I thought on Clinch, and the Battle of Splinterville—the trouble that come of it, really—it was all because that colonel *laughed* and rose to dust off the powder and said alright and unbuckled the thing, going so far as to hold out the scabbard, and I could see the day's frolic starting to unwind, many walking, pulling up their friends from the white snow, and pulling up their Enemies besides, it was not a time what seemed to me ripe for trouble. The dark was making it hard to fight on, with the lines now misshaped by the charges, all uniformed more or less alike, even more so as of being covered in the snow.

---

[49] Re: "play it by trust": Though in many ways it beggars the imagination, in a final, "last ditch" attempt at finding anachronism in the EW, Colflatt connects this passage to an art installation by Yoko Ono, first displayed in London's Indica Gallery in 1966, consisting of an all-white chess set. Entitled *Play It By Trust*, viewers were encouraged to sit and play. Naturally, after a few moves, it was impossible to remember which pieces belonged to which side. See Colflatt, "A 'Colonel' of Truth Unravels the 'Wrapper'," 390. Far from being a convincing "anachronism," it is in fact technically possible that Yoko Ono got the idea from Henry Wallace rather than the other way around, Professor Hirschorn having mentioned the "play it by trust" statement in his Fall, 1965 *Western Historical Yearbook* article on the wrapper one year before her exhibition. I think it *far* more likely that this very simple phrase had an independent invention by Ms. Ono and Pvt. Wallace. See Jules DeRossier, "Forensics and Colonels and Yoko--Oh No!: Researcher Wraps Up Edition of the 'Chickamauga Letter'." *Journal of the Center for Southeast Texas Studies*. 28 (Spring 1998), 78.

Your Clinch he was reaching out and gripping the scabbard, it looked to be a fine type of saber inside, and Clinch I could see was shaking, near jumping in a fever what did not match the occasion, and that Colonel paid no mind at first, but then he gripped back his sword, tugged it, as Clinch would not release. *What is this?* said that officer. *I will see an Officer* said this Carolinian, his own heat starting to rise almost as high as that of Clinch himself, and tugging on that scabbard to shake loose your boy. *I will yield to no Private*, and Clinch saying *You will Surrender*, and that officer coming back with *Let Go*, and *I Order You*, and *You let it Go* said Clinch, they tugged and hauled at each other, sir, it all going pretty much on in this manner between the two till Clinch called that man a shovel load of yeasty sh— and give a tug and got that sword and into his own paws sure.

It is a fact, sir, Ward and Mack and Donovan and I had to come in to grabble up Clinch, with Mack holding fast his feet and Ward clapping fast his mouth such that the stream of words what we knew him well capable of could not break forth, and Donovan give the colonel back the sword with a kind of bow, but that was not enough for that man who wanted *Names*. Him waving the sword around, pointing it at Clinch, pointing it at us, saying *Names, Names* until a swirl of snow come around—it had started in to fall again by then, sir, was wet and cold—and with Clinch kicking a fuss we drug him off, that colonel giving us a mad holler and calling for *Major Moffett, Major Moffett!* whoever that was,[50] us dragging him hard and Clinch making a weird path behind us almost like the one he dug down that slope in Louisiana, this time with his kicking feet what we finally put a stop to by the five of us together *lifting*—no easy task—pulling him up off the snow and him hollering *You have Surrendered to the Proud Porkers of the 1rst Arkansas*— yelling that through Ward's fingers—what was a good idea come to think of it—but we carried him off the snow so as

---

[50] If this call is for Maj. Robert C. Maffett, then the altercation could be with Col. James D. Nance, commander of the 3rd South Carolina Regiment, General Joseph Kershaw's Brigade.

not to leave something that *Major Moffett* or whoever that colonel sent after us could yet follow. I, for one, was unsure whether or not he, that colonel, might recognize us all later anyway, Clinch for sure, your boy being of such a unusual shape and form, snow-covered or no—while Ward kept trying to talk Clinch quiet, pointing out how he was almost coming to blows with a Commissioned Officer and you could not mistreat one of those save they was on the other side in what case they was more like fair game but still not completely. Clinch told us that sword was *his* and that he should have been able to at least hold it a while, him having captured that man fair, and that colonel being only just a man same as him, and we all sort of had doubts about that but little Clinch kicked and fussed more though we tried to stop him, and he said we all had the right to stupidity once and a while but was now abusing the privilege and should put him down and your boy called us maggot pies and clack dishes and dewberries besides but we was determined men, for this was not a funny situation. A moon come up to shine through the scant fall of snow—what I had never seen before, snow and moon at once—and this also caused more light as the sky though flaking [was yet cleared (?)] off into only fingerling sorts of clouds yet that light was not what we wanted as it would give that colonel or his troops a brighter way to trail us. Peacock thought it good to go back to our shacks through the brush where we could not be traced, so we strayed off into the way of the treeline, with the silence of these woods starting to bring us to more calm once we got among them. Of those men who pulled and cajoled and coerced your boy back through those trees that night they are no more save Mack and myself, our company now a thin ghost of that what whipped the Carolinians so sound.[51] We stopped there in the moonlight and leaned and

---

[51] 4,350 Texans served in Hood's Brigade from 1861 to 1865. Six hundred and two surrendered at Appomattox. (The un-reconstructable Hood personally never surrendered his troops or his sword.) Ramsey, *Lee's Grenadier Guards*, 255. Company B, 1rst Texas, was wiped out completely, with no survivor present at Appomattox out of

blew against the trunks a while, and that moon was so big it was big as a boiler snagged in the branches. We sank down to rest, Mack's bottom lip where he had been struck by one of the deadly clods starting to shake so much he looked a fright like a man about to cry. We stayed still, and Donovan smoked his pipe, but I saw that Mack was just shaking his head, and Ward said something about he wished Hock was still around that being his dead nigger's name who wasn't there to warm up the mess for us when we got back,[52] and the trouble with the colonel didn't seem so big no more, though Clinch he never forgot it, at that particular moment he was much calmer, and did not have to be held back to keep him from returning to that field to snatch *his* sword. It was a silly idea all the way, yet I rested and had my head on my own knees and though it is difficult to explain what happened next it is the truth, sir, that the five[53] of us out there in those woods with the big moon, we all started to weep at the same time, it was that Clinch first said something and . . . I can not, though I am trying hard, remember what it was he said though I think it might come—but whatever it was it started us laughing just a little bit, then Mack turned away his head, injured by a clod and all, yet his lips was quivering for more than that, and Ward went to comfort him but by then they was both themselves shaking, and I am not a overly sensitive type of man sir, what I doubt you are yourself, and that is a thing I point out not as any sort of critical reproach to the either of us, but I can gather something of your own Nature, I believe, by looking on Clinch's—for Clinch was one who could find a way to cast a cold eye on the most tearsome of spectacles like going through the things of them dead Enemies, like peering into their eyes deep as he did yesterday on the day of his own demise, and on that road full of men and parts of burnt men

---

a total of 102 members. *Ibid*, 341.

[52] The last mention of this figure in the EW. Hock could be short for "Hercules." Slaves were often given names from Greek and Roman antiquity.

[53] There are by my count six of them.

knee deep[54] and it is the case as well, I believe, that those among this world's citizens who come up with country ways with Farm Knowledge have a insight into the Unsentimental Life, its Meat and Juice, and how that can be forced out of its protecting skin into ugly contortions sometimes unbelievable (of course I am thinking, now, almost against my will, of that cow), and I am saying all only to show that this being the case, and all of us being Men and Men of Hard Type who even when we run from battle did always manly run yet this is no picture of imagination, sir, but rather a fact that *All* of us sat under them trees and under that moon, each with fixed expression, not of terror nor sorrow neither, Mack and Peacock, and Ward and Donovan and your now dead boy Michael and myself, we sat and cried, and I went through all these memories in a kind of a short second while I wandered on this field yesterday, and I turned over these memories in my mind while I wandered.

That cow, Splinterville, murder, the alligators thrashing, the strange weeper, and Holmes whose blood and brains I got on my face and hat[55] and more besides . . . after having thought about all this, I chanced on the true marrow of this day of Clinch's demise what is the reason I am writing now in the first place, and I must bring this to a close as soon the sun will rise and our new day's new work begin. Sir, I went weak and uncertain when it come to pass and did truly believe

---

[54] Likely a reference to Sharpsville/Antietem. Hood's Brigade took part in every major battle of the Eastern Theater save Chancellorsville, plus Chickamauga in the West.

[55] Although Colflatt places this man among the "just made up," Keith mentions a Hiram Holmes Bronson in Company L and lists him as "killed at Gaines Mill." *Hood's Texas Brigade*, 320. Colflatt notes as well that when it comes to Private Wallace and his squad having "a big boo hoo," something "simply does not feel right" to him. We must assume he's relying on his experiences with the 82nd Airborne here as a gauge. Still, Dr. Colflatt probably should not seek out and interpret evidence to make it align with his feelings, but rather start with the evidence before him, and build an argument from that. Colflatt, "This Time It's Personal. . ." 377. DeRossier, "You're Welcome to Your Own Opinion . . ." *passim*.

the fierce brandy was making me look at what Could Not Be, for there he was on a horseback, one foot rested over saddle leather, good arm above head, good hand grasping at limb of tree—John Bell Hood of course, sir, Major-General—yellow of beard, broad of shoulder, with spiking eyes what looked down and into everything, the Major-General sat his horse so and leaned on a high part of that tree, amongst a Y in the trunk, and grapeshot and minies zangered around him, d-mn all he cared, and he spoke to me.

What he truly said to me, sir, with his voice, was not so much, but I listened sharp and could not help but catch words between the words he used [because events(?)] had all slowed like they will in dream, where you can have experience of a week's travels, joys, and horror, yet awake and it be only a quarter hour since you dropped off, there you are right where you were, nodding in the kitchen, your mother shaking you gentle. And these words between the words of Hood sounded of Conflict, Clash and Disaccord—of Contumely, Biting, Tusselling, Yarrgh, Yarrgh, Yarrgh, and so on, and I saw future times. I was affected, sir, and that is why either I was in a state of mind to see future times or else I am just remembering what was soon to be future times in this way . . . what I mean is this: I remember I saw General Hood's leg about to go shatter and get carried off before it ever did, for such is what happened to our general in this place—like stolen goods, that leg of his, taken so quick.[56] That made me sad to think how such a thing yet to

---

[56] John Bell Hood suffered the loss of his right leg as a result of injury from a minie ball on the second day of Chickamauga. Strangely, although he commanded five divisions, he fell into the arms of the troops of the Texas Brigade which he had originally commanded on many other fields of battle. David H. Nutting, *Never Retreat: The Story of John Bell Hood*, (New Orleans, Garden Press: 1890), 102.

Though much is made of primitive field surgical conditions of the time and the resulting high casualty rate from amputation, officers were often able to get quite good private care. Hood survived and recuperated under the attentions of his own doctor and—minus his leg and the use of one arm—was thus fit to be tied onto a horse and dosed with laudanum from which vantage he could destroy his own

happen to his leg was going to be, till he spoke his phrase to me, words I heard as *Rhubarb, Set-To, Fight, Fight, Fight,* and it was then I come to know the nature of our Purpose and Clinch's too at this field, I saw ahead and knew ahead of time our Victory here.

John Bell Hood's powerful swift sword hung at one side slashed in curtains of red, and I saw then that this was what I had been hoping for and nothing else, a meeting with my old brigadier—seeing once again my old leader and the man I left home to fight for. I was of a sudden looking at him, him looking right back and smiling and he spoke to me of *War* then let go that limb above and started to prod at his teeth with a splinter, I think he must have just finished lunch and did not remember me at all, just took me to be a straggler.

And the fact was I should not have been so startled as all that to see him—Hood had joined up with the two-mile locomotive train and the rest of the Corps when we come through Richmond, rising from his cot though still not mended from his own Grievous Wound, I just did not know till later. He had gotten on the train, that was all, so while his being here showed as characteristic of his Gallantry and Daring, or maybe even his romantic disregarding as to Preservation of Self, it did not follow anything at all like those staggering fancies I was at that time knitting in my mind, like: General Hood had *ridden* from Virginia to Nth Georgia *on the mare,* just to be beside his men, or . . . that something like my vision of the Cow, I was seeing only some kind of *Heavenly Projection* of General Hood, meant for mine eyes alone. Besides, that Caesar-like curtained drape holding his

---

army a year and a half later at Franklin. See G. P. Beckman, *Home Front: Wealth and Poverty in the Confederacy,* (Chapel Hill, Smith Press, 1990). As an aside: both of the above volumes were first loaned to me by Alan Colflatt when we shared a dorm room at Port Arthur University. As another aside, Hood enlisted Arthur Collier, Co. H, 4th Texas with the dubious honor of shipping his severed right leg back to friends in the Lone Star State, although it is not known why he wanted them to keep it. Ramsey, *Lee's Grenadier Guards,* 322.

sword, it was really a sling and it held his smashed arm, I could see that with a moment's concentration, but there he was and he looked down at me and he opened his mouth and set me straight.

He said, —Boy, you stop that and go right up there right now.

I looked around myself. I had no blouse nor jacket, they was gone—I guess from when I was checking myself and looking for leaks—my belt and rifle was off somewheres, I was a shambles. I heard the inner tumult of his words, with *Riot, Turbulence* and *Ferment* among them, and I saw the future times, and said, —Yes, sir, and I vowed I would find out Clinch's folks and write to them only of course there is only you, sir, to write to explain the occurrence of your dead son's death, but first I had a bit of work to do, what your Clinch would have done better only now it was only me left to.

I turned back to find my Company, and I do not know how but I did find them, I stumbled over Mack somehow, and then both Pard and the 3rd Captain strode up to me, that officer with a bad shot through his hand—what somehow made me feel better of him—and Old Pard wanting to know for what was I being so controversial, why had I thrown down my weapon, so I explained I needed a weapon as much as a squirrel had need of a hat, and then Mack asked what did a squirrel have to do with it and why had I taken leave of my blouse, my cartridge belt, boots, did they catch fire or what?—but to me such a question smacked of inopportunity.[57]

I could not heed those around me, but set off to the line of them our Tormentors straight to tell them a thing or two on matters about what they, no doubt, had some Degree of Confusion—it was so obvious I got disappointed in myself, I had not needed the gallant Major-General to

---

[57] Skeptics might wonder how Wallace could find his company so quickly in the chaos of this morning, but should recall that the 4th got too far ahead in its mad dash to follow Hood's orders and had to retreat. It is likely that the company found Wallace rather than the other way around. O.R.A. Series I, Vol 30, Part II, p. 511.

set me right, him with his leg about to go *kerplow*—I could
have come to these conclusions alone by looking in my own
mind (I was very tired, though, I wanted to get this done,
quick, and take a nap)—only by pursuing my own Natural
Patterns of Thought I could have concluded just that what
the General had showed: that this was no conversation nor
song nor teetering balance, but more it was only what was
set before me and was real—I was separating the dream
times from the real times, sir, having come to a firm hold on
the latter and truly gotten woke up from the former—and
realizing all: that what this was was a *Quarrel of Animosity.*

Because while things was still around me breathing
and braying I saw now that the hill was not singing down
on the valley it was shouting it down and saying come on
rise up make something of yourself, and the fields was not
humming but whining and cajoling as they did not want to
bother to rise and in fact was willing that hill to fall flat and
die, and that the horizon cut in the cooling breeze what run
over it and made the air go red from invisible blood what
stained the cloud fringe in a drool, and that at night the stars
you lie on ground to watch with twig between your teeth all
have elbowed each other aside to get to be the ones in front,
and so to the honor of Clinch who had joined in this fracas
and give all, to his cantankerous memory, and to the honor
of General Hood's leg what perhaps at that moment was
getting all broke up (but why should a Man so Grand as that
have supporting need for anything so Everyday?) and to the
honor of this our Certain and Deadly Victory what I could
see bloomed before us even before it got in the papers—a
Victory so Great I doubt we can ever survive another like
it[58]—I went past that line of my own company to a narrow
footpath, straight to a tree-edge at the top of a beak of soil,
and this act must have been taken by that Enemy crouched
up there in a angry mob as a surprising one as at first they
responded not at all.

---

[58] Union casualties at Chickamauga: 1,657 killed, 9,756 wounded,
4,757 captured/missing. Confederate casualties: 2,312 killed, 14,674
wounded, 1,468 captured/missing.

I give it to them, Mr. Williamson, and told them the way it lay, letting them know what I wanted them to. I tried to shape in advance the proper form of contumely to hurl and I run through in my mind what would Clinch say, it would have something to do with their physical makeup, ancestry for sure would play a part, [the] lack as to their degrees of [intellect(?)], and as I come on I could start to see them, their heads out from behind trunks, over cut-down logs, their faces like corn cobs, not the usual kind but the Indian kind where each segment is another color, so I thought I might somehow include that in the insult: —Hey corn-heads, or such. The world wheeled under. Flags snapped in the breezes and I got close enough to hear the angry snaps. The sun is now rising, the light is coming and I have to get it down now and tell you that I wanted to light into them right and hard, sir, throw something sweltering, what would make me feel a big man, how would Clinch do it? But nothing I could think of felt strong enough, so I started off thinking up some just basic curses comparing them, our Enemy, to Barnyard Animal Breeds, and this I planned to augment further once I could get up in their midst by adding offenses regarding their A—holes—that orifice being such a affixed favorite among your dear dead boy's dear themes—

—and I have thought of it now! That is it! That is what Clinch said in those woods when we all panted in the snow. And it was about that moon, that big moon, and was simple: *If you think this moon is big you should see the one we got in Bold Springs!* —and how my thoughts was of him and you, too, sir, as I tramped up that hillside, and I hoped I could just start with one good one, one scorcher, of a Clinch-like nature, for with one then the others would roll out with their flames as they did for Clinch himself, and I would be able to end in a exultation and flourish of Jeer, Heckle and Affront, but by the time I got close all I was able to say was what I did what was: —Go away you! and if you read the newspapers you will know this is what they did so that must have been good enough though Clinch doubtless could have done lots more.

Thousands of them, sir, fled all out of there that afternoon, prodded at also by a assault of a full division under Bushrod Johnson what went at that hill at that same time, but still that night we had their stores and guns, we burned their wagons and sipped their whiskey, and I kneel under one of their blankets and watch the smoke and stars disappear with come of day, and the 3rd Captain wanted to know what did I do this for, this seemed to him to be some kind of uncalled-for hostility on my part (Think of that one, sir. *Think* of it!), though I really could not even get it all straight till writing it now to you.[59]

For truth is, it is so hard to sit like this and not go after them some more. It has passed now yet to another day and the only way I can relieve my head, it feels yet so stuffed and un-oriented from that brandy, is to cast back my eyes and look into the smoke and the sky, and all this waiting . . . it is just a eternity of waiting, sir, till we can move and I can make my natural Cause of tearing into and Denouncing and scorning again. It is all because of your dead boy, Mr. Williamson, that I know this, and because of Major-General John Bell Hood, and the way he told me *Go right up there right now* and pointed his toothpick at that hill. Right up that hill's where I went, sir, as would have Clinch if he was here, as would anyone, as would you.

I am hoping this gives you some good feelings toward your son and his last days and his inspiration, and I am

---

[59] Informed readers will recognize that the author is skipping over, was not present at, or, perhaps, was merely unconscious during the important events that took place during the afternoon and on into the evening of Sept. 20. While it is true that the successful assault on Snodgrass Hill probably assured Confederate victory at Chickamauga, General George Henry Thomas's fierce defense of the high ground north of that area allowed the bulk of the Union army to retreat into Chattanooga. The South's success at Chickamauga Creek, not pursued by any movement on the part of commanding General Braxton Bragg, proved to be ultimately without strategic value. See Paul Cameron, *The Rock: George Henry Thomas in the West,* (New York, Discovery Press, 1992) *passim.*

sending in addition also this the cartridge belt[60] of Clinch's what was the only thing of value we found on him when we buried him today on that Field of Triumph, we kept his spectacles on him as he looked no Clinch without them. I am sure you will want to keep a keepsake of a Great Man who is now gone to Greater Things after performing well his part in this Dispute and hope the belt will serve. There was 4 bitter acorns in his pocket, but those I ate in his memory.

With respect and admiration,
Pvt. Henry Oldham Wallace, C.S.A.

---

[60] Here is revealed, for any willing to read to the end of it, the item bundled inside Henry Wallace's "Equinox Wrapper."

BIOGRAPHICAL NOTE:

Cliff Hudder teaches English at Montgomery College in Conroe, Texas. An MFA graduate of the University of Houston, his stories have appeared in *Alaska Quarterly Review*, *The Kenyon Review*, and *The Missouri Review* among other publications, and his work has received the Barthelme Award, the Michener Award, the Peden Prize, and the Brazos Bookstore Short Story Award from the Texas Institute of Letters. *Splinterville* is his first book.